STEPS INTO THE PAST...

He handed me the gun, and while I was getting the heft of it he opened a drawer and pulled out a shoulder holster. He told me to take off my jacket, strapped the thing in place over my shirt. The gun slid into it easily. I flattered myself that with a little practice I could make it slip out just as easily – but whether or not I'd have it pointing in the right direction after I'd slipped it out was another matter.

'And a side holster,' I said.

'Damn it all, Johnnie, do you think I'm fitting you out to fight a private war?'

'Yes.'

'But what do you want a side holster for?'

'You told me that I might have to work in a spacesuit; that's why you wanted me for the job.'

'There's still time to back out, John.'

'I'll stick,' I said.

Also by A. Bertram Chandler in Sphere Books

THE RIM OF SPACE
WHEN THE DREAM DIES

Bring Back Yesterday
A. BERTRAM CHANDLER

SPHERE BOOKS LIMITED
30/32 Gray's Inn Road, London WC1X 8JL

First published in Great Britain by
Allison & Busby Ltd 1981
Copyright © 1961 by Ace Books, Inc.
Published by Sphere Books Ltd 1982

TRADE
MARK

This book is sold subject to the condition that
it shall not, by way of trade or otherwise, be lent,
re-sold, hired out or otherwise circulated without
the publisher's prior consent in any form of
binding or cover other than that in which it is
published and without a similar condition
including this condition being imposed on the
subsequent purchaser

Set in Times

Printed and bound in Great Britain by
Cox & Wyman Ltd, Reading

To Susan Legree

Chapter One

I AWOKE with a start, with the frightening conviction that something was dreadfully wrong. It was, I decided, the silence. The thin, high keening of the interstellar drive is so much part of a spaceman's life that its abrupt cessation is more shocking than the sudden cacophony of alarm bells and sirens. *But why hadn't the alarm been sounded?* Not only was the drive silent but so were the sobbing pumps, the whining fans.

But there were other sounds.

There was someone breathing gently. I held my own breath for a few seconds, established the fact that it was not my own respiration to which I was listening. There was the ticking of a clock. And — faint, muffled — there were other noises. I tried to identify them. There was a distant, screaming roar that I knew, somehow, was far overhead. There were not so distant mechanical growlings and purrings. There was the sudden knowledge — it should have been comforting, but it was not — that it was the pulsebeat of a city that I was hearing, not that of a ship.

I moved uneasily in the bed — a bed, not a narrow bunk — and felt a woman's body, soft yet firm, warm, smooth, against my own. The contact should have been stimulating, but it was not. The situation, which should have been beautifully right, was still dreadfully wrong. I groped for the switch of the bedside lamp — the lamp that we had left turned on until, exhausted, we had fallen into a deep sleep. I could remember, now, summoning my last reserves of energy to switch the light off.

I pressed the switch. The soft, amber light was kind to my eyes. It was reflected from the sleek, auburn hair against the white pillow, from the smooth shoulder, from the golden curve of her back. It illumined the dial of the wall clock, the black hands and numerals showing up with startling, frightening clarity.

"Ilona!" I said sharply.

She replied with a sound that was half purr, half grunt, stirred, pulled the sheet and the light blanket over her bare shoulders, more than half over her head.

"Ilona!"

This time she did not reply.

I shook her, gently at first, then more urgently. She turned to face me, her eyes opening slowly, reluctantly, startlingly blue under the dark hair.

She said, "It's you. . . ."

She said, peevishly, "Can't you let a girl sleep?"

"That clock . . ." I began.

"What about it?" She started to slide again under the bedclothes.

"Is it right?"

"Of course it's right."

I jumped out of the bed, walked swiftly to the window. I remembered that she had shown me, the previous evening, the polarization controls. I turned the dial and the black, featureless expanse of glass became translucent, then cloudily transparent and then crystal clear. Bright sunlight streamed into the bedroom.

"Have you no consideration?" she complained.

I ignored her, looked over New Prague, at the tall shining buildings, the gleaming, artificial lakes, the green parks. To the northeast was the spaceport, and looking towards it I was looking into the sun. Nevertheless I could make out the gleaming spire that was the control tower, the tall, oddly convoluted columns of the Carlotti Beacons. There should have been another tower there, another gleaming spire, but I couldn't see it.

But, at this time, that other tower should not have been there in any case.

I knew then, and the knowledge was a dreadful emptiness more dreadful than a first tripper's first experience of free fall. I *knew*, but I had to be sure. I walked slowly to the telephone, opened the book that was on the table beside the instrument, found the number of the spaceport control, punched the combination. The screen came alive and an attractive girl looked out at me from behind the circular transparency. Her eyebrows lifted at the sight of my nakedness but she said, calmly enough, "Spaceport inquiries here. Can I help you, sir?"

"What are you playing at?" came a muffled voice from the bed.

I ignored it. "The *Lightning*," I said. "Has she blasted off yet?"

"Of course, sir. At 0830 hours. She was half an hour behind schedule."

"Thank you," I muttered, switching off.

"Have you quite finished?" demanded the voice from beneath the huddle of bedclothes.

I hadn't.

I punched another combination, found myself facing another attractive girl. She, like the girl in the spaceport office, was blonde and attractive, but, obviously, far more used to dealing with callers in a state of undress. Or, it could be she was more broad-minded.

"Exchange," she cooed. "Good morning, sir."

"It's not."

"Is anything wrong, sir?"

"Yes. Do you keep a record of early morning calls?"

"We do, sir."

"Did you call this number," I glanced at the numerals printed on the card on the punchboard, repeated them, "at 0530 hours this morning?"

"Hold the line, sir." Her eyes were downcast, her brow slightly furrowed, as she consulted some sort of record. "Yes, sir. The number was called. There was an acknowledgement."

"Thank you."

"Now can I get some sleep?" Ilona asked coldly.

"No!" I almost shouted.

I strode to the bed, pulled the light coverings from her. She sat upright, glaring at me. She was beautiful, but her beauty failed to register. She was no more than an

3

arrangement of arms and legs and breasts that, although aesthetically satisfactory, was without real significance. I was beginning to hate her.

"Do you realize what's happened?" I shouted.

She winced. "Please be quiet. You aren't aboard your ship now, bellowing orders."

I said, "I never shall be aboard a ship again."

She asked, without much interest, "What do you mean?"

I said, "I've missed my ship, and you know what that means."

She became more aware of me. She pulled up the sheet so that it covered her. She repeated my words tonelessly. "You missed your ship. . . ."

"Yes. Damn it all, Ilona, what happened last night?"

She laughed. "You should know. You were here too."

"But what happened? I rang the Exchange myself, asking for a call at 0530 hours. That would have given me ample time to get out to the Spaceport. I checked with the girl, and she assures me that the call was made, and acknowledged."

She laughed again. "That's funny, darling. I seem to remember a vague sort of dream about getting out of bed to answer the phone."

"Damn it!" I swore. "This is serious. Don't you realize what you've done?"

"What *I've* done?" she countered. "Don't forget that you were quite keen on trying the euphorine, even after I'd warned you of the possible consequences."

"But you assured me that you'd taken the stuff so many times that you were practically immune."

"Did I, darling? But I've been away from home a long time and I've been cut off from supplies. And I've been told that in such cases immunity vanishes, that a person such as myself is even less immune than somebody trying euphorine for the first time. But, after all, I *did* get up to answer the phone."

"Ilona, this is serious."

She started to laugh again, then thought better of it. "Go through to the bathroom," she told me. "You'll find a bottle in the cabinet — anti-euphorine. Bring it through, with a glass."

I did as she told me, finding the bottle without difficulty. When I got back into the bedroom she was up, standing naked before the big window, letting the sunlight play over her slim body. She turned, smiling, murmuring, "The sun is my only true lover. . . ."

I kept my eyes on her face, said, "Here's the bottle."

She sighed, "Must I?"

I began to wish that the effects of the drug had persisted in my case. I asked, "What do I do with this?"

She smiled impishly, replying, "Unluckily I'm too much of a lady to give the correct answer." Then: "If you really must, pour just three drops into the glass."

I did so, handed her the goblet. She raised it to her lips and drained it, shuddering slightly. She let the glass fall, walked rapidly to where her robe was hanging over a chair, shrugged herself into it. The heavy black material covered her from neck to ankle, from shoulder to wrist. Over it her face was white and hard.

She said, "Get something on. Then you'd better get out of here."

I was suddenly conscious of my own nakedness. I found slacks and shirt, climbed into them, my back to her. Then I turned to face her. "Ilona," I said, "this is quite a jam I'm in."

"This is quite a jam you're in," she agreed.

"My career . . ." I said.

"You told me," she remarked coldly, "that you were tired of being a spaceman. Well, now's your big chance to be something else."

"But what?"

"That's your problem." She walked to the bedside table, took a cigarette from the box, drew sharply on the cylinder to ignite it. Her narrowed eyes regarded me through the wreathing smoke. "That's your problem. I suggest that you get out of here, buy yourself a morning paper and start looking through the classified ads for a job."

"But. . . ."

Her voice rose. "Get out, I said. You needn't think that I'm going to keep you, that I'm going to supply you with free board and lodging. You got yourself into this mess; get yourself out of it, if you can. On your bicycle, spaceman. Hit the track."

I spoke slowly and carefully. "I suppose that I'm allowed to use your bathroom before I go?"

"Don't be too long," she said.

I used the bathroom.

I was noisily sick first of all and felt a little better. Then I took a shower, washing the scent of her from my skin. I used the tube of depilatory cream in the cabinet, then dressed again. Back in the bedroom, while she watched silently, I put on my socks and shoes, my necktie, my jacket.

"Ilona," I said.

"Goodbye," she said tonelessly.

I let myself out of the apartment, rode the cushion of compressed air in the drop shaft down to ground level.

Chapter Two

YOU'VE PROBABLY read about the utter loneliness of deep space.

Let me tell you this. When it comes to utter loneliness, deep space isn't in the running with a city in which you know nobody, have no home to go to, from which your ship, with your familiar little cabin and the familiar faces of your shipmates, has blasted off.

But, I thought, perhaps the girl at the inquiry desk was wrong. Perhaps *Lightning* hasn't blasted off. Perhaps she is still waiting for me.

Then I despised myself for my wishful thinking. Even if Captain Gruen had liked me, which he hadn't, he was too fervid a worshipper of the sacred schedule ever to delay the departure of his vessel for more than a bare half hour. And, even though second mates are a fairly important cog in the machinery of a big ship, they are not indispensable. I knew what must have happened. Wahlgren, the third, would now be acting-second. The fourth would be acting-third, the fifth would be acting-fourth and young Lewisham, senior cadet, would now be acting-fifth. And *Lightning,* the latest and most luxurious Trans-Galactic Clipper, would be falling down the light years, well on her way to Port of Spain, Caribbea, her next port of call.

I slowed down.

There was no hurry. The ship was gone. Furthermore, I had to decide where first to go. The spaceport? But I had only a few dollars in my pocket and a taxi fare would take most of what I had. But there, almost ahead of me, was the entrance to a subway station. I began to walk towards it and then asked myself, But what do I do when I get there? Weep salt tears on to the blast scars on the concrete?

I stood there, ignoring the occasional snarl from passers-by whose way I was impeding. As yet, I wasn't thinking very well. This may have been the result of exhaustion, or of shock, or of the aftereffects of the euphorine. Or all three. Not that it particularly mattered.

Next door to the subway station was a small cafe.

It was a cheerful place, too cheerful, its walls covered with abstract designs in which scarlet and lemon-yellow predominated. The music from the wall speakers was also too cheerful. I shuddered slightly but made my way to a table, sat down. The waitress was typically Carinthian, her Siamese-cat sleekness clad in tapering black slacks, with a vividly green garment above them that could almost have been no more than a coat of paint. I looked at her without enthusiasm. I had had women in a big way — Carinthian women especially.

"Coffee," I said, without looking at the menu she was holding open before me. "And buttered toast."

"White or black, sir?"

"Black."

"Harz or imported?"

Damn the woman! Why did she have to keep on muttering?

"Harz," I said, thinking that the locally grown product must be cheaper than that ferried all the way from distant Earth. When she was gone I glanced at the menu and found that my assumption had been wrong — but the economics of interstellar commerce have always been a mystery to me.

But so far. I thought, an additional twenty cents doesn't matter very much. I sipped the hot, bitter brew, nibbled a finger of buttered toast. I listened to the light, morning music that was coming from the wall speakers. The band, wherever it was — at the local broadcasting station or in some recording studio far away in space and time? — was playing a medley of the so-called Spacemen's Marches which, as you probably know, are old, old melodies with modern words tacked on to them. I realized that I was singing softly to myself:

"Goodbye, I'll run to seek another sun
Where I may find
There are hearts more kind than the ones left behind . . ."

I stopped singing abruptly, nibbled more toast, sipped more coffee. I thought, That's all very well. One can run to seek another sun, another planetary system, only if one has the wherewithal to pay one's fare or the professional qualifications making one eligible for employment aboard a spaceship.

I thought, but I still have the qualifications. The Old Man is sure to have had my papers landed along with the rest of my effects. And spacemen aren't so plentiful that missing a ship leads to automatic cancellation of a certificate. Even so, there's the black list. I'm finished as far as T.G. Clippers are concerned. And none of the other big concerns — Interstellar Transport Commission, Waverley Royal Mail, Cluster Lines — will look at me. There's Rim Runners, of course. They'll take anybody who's still warm and can flash some kind of a certificate. But even if I wanted the Rim, which I don't, I'd have to get out there first.

"Some more coffee, sir?" asked the girl.

"No," I growled, adding a belated "Thank you." Then: "I wonder if you could tell me the way to the Trans-Galactic Clipper offices?"

"Turn right when you leave here," she said. "After three blocks you come to Masaryk Square. You'll find the offices of all the interstellar lines there, on the far side."

I thanked her, went out into the bright, unwarming sunlight, the chilly breeze.

I was feeling a little better after the coffee and toast, a little stronger. I was tempted to stop at one of the bars on the way to the Square to continue the process of revivification, but decided against it. I had met Maleter, T.G.'s Branch Manager, and I had not liked him. But now I could not afford to antagonize him and would have to fight down the strong temptation to tell him what to do with the entire T.G. fleet, stern vanes and all.

I slowed my pace again, telling myself that I had done so the more to appreciate my surroundings. This was the first time that I had seen New Prague by day — from ground level, that is. And I had never seen much of it by night either. The previous evening, for example, I had taken a taxi straight from the spaceport to the apartment house in which Ilona lived.

So that was my story, and I stuck to it, although I knew that the real reason was to postpone the evil half hour by a few minutes. Maleter would not be pleased to see me. Correction: He would be pleased to see me. Maleter, who made no secret of his dislike for spacemen, would be pleased to have one of the breed on his carpet, figurative cap in hand.

I walked slowly, looking to right and left.

New Prague was a fine city. On either side of the broad avenue toward the buildings, each of them standing in its own park of greenery and gay flower beds. To one like myself, born and reared on overcrowded Earth, this seemed a criminal waste of space, but the effect was pleasing. Galleries ran around the towers at various levels and graceful bridges connected them.

The street was thronged with private cars, another strange sight to the Earthling eye. The majority of them were mono-cars, running on the stored power of their huge flywheels, but there were a number of hovercraft. And overhead flitted the swarms of gaily coloured taxis.

There were plenty of foot passengers too. Once again I found myself comparing this world with my home planet, and not to Earth's advantage. These people were well-fed and well-clad, the men inclined to stoutness, the women tall and sleek and attractive. They had never eaten synthetics, had never awakened gasping in the night, brought to near anoxia by the failure of the city ventilating fan. Like the majority of spacemen, like most of those freed by luck or circumstances from the vast, squalid slum that is Earth, I had tended to despise the people of my own world. Now, a stranger among the elegant, arrogant crowds of this one-time colony, I began to feel a certain nostalgia for my beginnings.

I walked around the Square.

The offices of the shipping lines were easy enough to find. On any world whatsoever they run to a pattern. Stone spaceships they are called, although they may be of stone, or of ferroconcrete, or of steel and glass, or of aluminium and plastic. Invariably their needle spires are aimed at the sky and, at their bases, architecturally unnecessary buttresses simulate vaned landing gear. From gaffs set high on their structure flutter the houseflags of the companies.

I looked for the T.G. flag — the stylized golden, old-time windjammer, all sails set, on the dark blue ground — and found it. I walked to the big, swinging doors, pushed through them into the building. The ground floor was one big office, broken up by the long, highly polished counters behind which relatively unimportant members of the staff worked. Slim fingers and gleaming nails were flashing over the keyboards of comptometers and typewriters, soft, carefully modulated voices speaking into voicewriters. Heavy male faces over broad shoulders nodded behind littered desks, frowning over matters of galactic moment such as, I thought, the alleged short shipment of one case of rum consigned from Port of Spain, Caribbea, to Port Tauber, Carinthia.

I ignored the glowing posters designed to lure intending travellers to glamorous, faraway planets, but read the signs: Galactic Passages, Outward Freight, Inward Freight, Claims. I found the one that I was looking for: Inquiries. It was over a little glass sentry box, all by itself in the middle of the vast expanse of floor.

There was a girl sitting in the box. She flashed me a professional smile as I approached and, even though that smile was one of the things that she was paid for, I appreciated it. She murmured, almost intimately, the inevitable, "Can I help you?"

"You can," I told her.

The smile stayed in place as she asked, "But how?"

Promising, I thought. Very promising. . . . Not without regret I told her, "I would like to see Mr Maleter."

"Have you an appointment?"

"No. But I think he'll be expecting me."

"Whom shall I say is calling?"

"Mr Petersen."

"Mr Peterson."

"Mr Peter*sen*."

"I'm sorry," she said, still smiling.

"That's all right."

I watched her punching the numbered buttons on the punchboard. Suddenly I thought, Her hands are like Ilona's, and there's something of Ilona in the shape of her head. . . . I thought viciously, Damn Ilona. . . .

The girl was looking into the screen, the back of which was towards me. Her face was serious now, unsmiling. I saw her flinch slightly. I heard the harsh voice, "Yes? What is it?"

"A Mr Petersen to see you, sir. He said that you were expecting him."

"Petersen? I don't know any Petersen."

"But he said —"

"Petersen?" The voice was harsher now. "Yes, of course. Send him up."

I heard the click as the connection was broken.

The girl raised her head. There was no trace of the professional smile; it had been replaced by unprofessional sympathy. She said, "Mr Maleter will see you now. The elevators are on your left. Get off at the fifth floor." She paused, then added, "Good luck."

I walked to the elevators with a swagger that did not reflect my true feelings.

Grey-clad, grey-faced, Maleter sat behind his desk of grey metal in a grey room. As I walked slowly over the wide expanse of grey carpet I was acutely conscious of the incongruous splash of colour that my clothing would be making; attire that had been donned as being suitable for a gay night ashore, that was absolutely unsuitable for a business call. I suppose, I thought, that this can be classed as a business call. . . .

Maleter's hard face was expressionless, could have been cast from the same material as the desk behind which he was sitting. I remembered all the things that I had heard about him. Iron Man Maleter, I had heard him called. Iron Man Maleter, the robot that walks like a man. Iron Man Maleter, who had said more than once, that only machines could run machines efficiently and that the ideal spaceman should regard himself, and be regarded as a machine. I remembered Hales, our Chief Officer, saying, "If that bastard ever gets to head office and becomes general manager there'll be a flood of resignations, both ashore and aspace, and mine'll be among them."

"Mr Petersen?" he said harshly.

"Guilty," I said.

He said, "Your humour is misplaced — although you are, in fact, guilty. You delayed the departure of one of our ships by no less than twenty-nine minutes, thirty-five seconds. Unluckily there is not yet in existence any legal machinery by which you may be adequately penalized."

He made a steeple of his hands, stared at me over them. His eyes, too, were grey, as were his brows and his hair.

I said nothing.

He asked, "Have you nothing to say for yourself?"

I told him, "No."

A faint flicker of expression crossed his face. Disappointment?

He said, "Mr Petersen, you are a disgrace to your service. The company considers itself fortunate in numbering you no longer among its employees. That is all." His voice rose slightly: "Get out."

"Mr Maleter —"

"I told you to leave."

"My gear, my personal effects."

"They were landed, I believe, care of the shipping master out at the spaceport."

"And my back pay?"

The metallic eyebrows lifted.

"Mr Petersen, surely you are not so naive as to believe that you have any further claims upon Trans-Galactic Clippers? I am well aware that some shipmasters are so weak as to make financial provision for deserters — Captain Gruen, in fact, wished to do so in your case. But I can assure you that this will never be allowed in any port over which I exercise jurisdiction. Legally, a spaceman who misses his ship forfeits all monies due to him, unless he can prove that his failure to rejoin was through no fault of his own. I do not think, Mr Petersen, that you can so prove?"

Neither do I, I decided regretfully.

"As a citizen of this planet," he went on, "I am naturally desirous that it be kept free of undesirables." He frowned, obviously blaming me for his slight lapse of syntax. "I have already been in touch with the Terran Consul. You will report to him and you will register as a D.T.S., Distressed Terran Spaceman. He will make arrangements for your board and lodging until such time as you can be shipped away aboard a suitable vessel.

"Get out."

To have said anything would have involved the loss of what few shreds of dignity remained to me.

I got out.

Chapter Three

THE TERRAN CONSUL may have been pleased to see me — as a matter of fact, although not in that official capacity, he was — but he succeeded in disguising his feelings remarkably well.

He kept me waiting for all of an hour on a hard bench in his outer office, with nothing to look at but his receptionist and a few ancient and tattered periodicals — *The Australian Coal, Shipping & Steel Monthly*, *The Californian Mortician's Gazette*, and the like. Even so, the magazines were the lesser of the two evils. Like them, the receptionist was obviously an import from Imperial Earth, and the importation must have taken place at least two decades in the past. Some Earth-women, having escaped from the drabness of the home planet, blossom exotically; some don't. This one hadn't. Furthermore something must have happened to her during her passage to Carinthia — or, perhaps, nothing had happened — as a result of which she disliked and distrusted spacemen. Conversation was impossible. She sat behind her desk glaring at me, her bony fingers busy with the knitting of some frowsy garment, and something that would be, when it was finished, as dreary and shapeless as the thing that she was wearing over her baggy and hairy tweed skirt.

At last there was a brief buzz on some sort of office intercom. She barely glanced up, raised her voice a little so that it was audible over her clicking needles, said, "The Colonel will see you now."

"Thank you," I said.

She ignored me. I got up and walked through to the inner office.

The Consul was a little man, fat, pink and bald. His eyes should have been pink too, but they were not; they were pale-blue, enormously magnified by his spectacles. He looked at me coldly.

"Yes, my man?"

"Petersen's the name," I told him.

"Yes, my man. I am aware of that." His pudgy hands shuffled the papers on his desk. "You are the deserter. From the Trans-Galactic Clipper *Lightning*."

"Not a deserter, sir. I missed my ship."

"You missed your ship. Precisely. You are a deserter."

"Legally speaking," I told him, "desertion can be presumed to have taken place only when a spaceman has left the ship with all his personal effects."

"You're a space lawyer, my man. I warn you, I'll not tolerate legal quibbles."

"I'm not a deserter," I said again. "And I think that it's essential that my legal status be made quite clear."

He snorted. "You have no status, my man, except that of a bloody nuisance. I have to see that you are fed and have a roof over your head until such time as a suitable ship comes in." His temper subsided. "Yes, a ship. There's *Delta Eridani*, in three weeks' time, for Earth via Caribbea, Van Diemen's Planet and Atlantia. . . ." He dealt himself a fresh hand from the untidy papers. He smiled smugly. "But do you wish to return to Earth?"

"I thought that I had no option."

"There may be one, my man. The Rim Worlds, for example, are crying out for certified space officers, even for officers who have blotted their copy books. In a month's time we have *Epsilon Puppis*, outward bound for Ultimo, Thule, Faraway and Lorn. . . ."

" 'Divine Bokhara,' " I quoted, " 'happy Samarkand, and the cities of the far northeast.' "

"What?" he demanded, goggling. "What?"

"Hassen," I told him. "Flecker, James Elroy."

"I don't know what you're talking about," he said sulkily.

"No matter. There are affairs of greater moment. Where, for example, do I sleep? When do I eat?"

"I had assumed," he said snottily, "that you would not be quite destitute."

"I am," I told him, stretching the truth only slightly. "The original Destitute Terran Spaceman, that's me." I didn't feel that I was accepting charity in letting Imperial Earth foot a few bills. I'd paid plenty to Imperial Earth in taxes.

He found a paper at the bottom of the heap. "You are booked in," he said, "at the Spaceman's Hostel, out at Port Tauber. I believe that your effects are there, too."

"And how do I get there?" I asked. "It's rather far to walk."

He looked at me with a pained expression, found a receipt pad among the litter. He scribbled something on it, pushed it and a twenty-five-cent-piece across to me. He said, "Your subway fare to the spaceport, my man. Will you sign, please?"

He was annoyed when I asked him for the loan of his pen. My own, I hoped, would be with my effects out at

Port Tauber. I signed.

He said, "Think it over, my man, about the Rim Worlds."

A sudden thought struck me. "Are you their Consul, too?" I asked.

"Agent," he admitted.

"Oh." Then another thought struck me. "What do I do for spending money?"

"Spending money? But the Hostel supplies board and lodging. And there are do-it-yourself laundry facilities."

"What about an occasional drink and smoke?"

"Really, my man, don't you think that you have forfeited all claim to such luxuries?"

"Perhaps, but. . . ."

The Consul dealt himself yet another hand of assorted papers, played an official-looking document like the ace of trumps. "If you care to sign this contract, my man, an advance of salary will be in order."

I looked at the sheet of heavy paper, saw the winged wheel embossed at the head of it. I read some of the print, not bothering with the small stuff. It was a contract. If I signed it, it would bind me to the service of Rim Runners for three years, Galactic Standard. I didn't like it. I didn't want to commit myself. But I wondered how I should feel when the last cigarette had been smoked, when the last of my few remaining dollars had been spent on the little luxuries without which life is hardly worth living.

I asked, "My status. My status as a Distressed Terran Spaceman. Does that prevent me from seeking employment on this planet?"

"No," he admitted at last. "Although Carinthia is no longer a member of Federation, Earthmen have full citizenship rights." He brightened. "But what employment can you find? You are skilled in one trade only. And unskilled labour on Carinthia is invariably hard manual work. You've spent most of your life in free fall. You could never stand sustained, physical labour." He beamed at me. "You'd better sign."

"I'll think about it," I told him.

I pocketed his — or was it Imperial Earth's? or the Rim Government's? — twenty-five cents and left the office.

I rode glumly in the subway out to Port Tauber, carefully boarding a non-smoking carriage so that I should not deplete my small store of cigarettes. From the Port Tauber station I rode the moving ramp that would carry me to the administration section. There, without difficulty, I found the shipping office.

The shipping master, like most of those who depend upon spaceborne commerce for a livelihood, regarded spacemen, especially such spacemen as have been unlucky enough to miss ships, as a nuisance. He scowled at me, demanded proof of identity — luckily I always carry my Guild Membership Card on my person — then threw a couple of closely typewritten sheets at me. I skimmed through their subject matter:

>I.S.S. *Lightning*
>At Port Tauber
>23-10-03 (Galactic)

Personal Effects of John Petersen, late Second Officer, landed to care of Superintendent, Government Shipping Office, Port Tauber:

One suitcase, containing:

Shirts, uniform	4 no.
Shorts, uniform	4 prs.
Sandals, uniform	1 pr.
Jackets, uniform	2 no.
Slacks, uniform	2 prs.
Shoes, uniform	2 prs.
Jackets, uniform, mess	1 no.

One briefcase, containing:
Certificate of Competency, Master Astronaut   1 no.

"I haven't all day to waste," barked the shipping master.

"All right. Where's my gear?"

"Here. Behind the counter. Better come through to get it."

"Is it far to the Hostel?"

"No. Just on the other side of the apron."

I looked out of the window, across the wide, wide expanse of blast-scarred concrete, all the wider and more desolate looking for the present absence of shipping.

"If you don't get a move on," said the official, "you'll have to go all the way round. The Moon Rocket's due in half an hour."

I looked at my heavy baggage and sighed audibly. The shipping master relented, grudgingly. "If you ask in the Porters' Lodge," he told me, "they might lend you a handtruck."

So I asked nicely in the Porters' Lodge. The head porter offered me more than a handtruck; he offered me the sympathy that, so far, had been in short supply on this planet. He insisted upon accompanying me across the field, helping to push the truck and maintaining a nonstop stream of chatter.

"They're too strict these days, lad, altogether too strict. Time was when a spaceman was expected to have a bit of old devil in him. I used to be a spaceman myself once — Sergeant of Marines, Survey Service. I remember when little Jimmy Carstairs — Commodore Carstairs he is now — missed his ship. He was just a sub-lieutenant at the time. On Caribbea, it was. We'd put in for recreation, then we got a hurry-up blast-off order to go and do something about the *Alpha Draconis* mutiny. Jimmy heard the recall siren all right — everybody on the whole damn planet must have heard it — but he was busy. Then when he'd finished being busy, it was too late. The old *Discovery* was already belting upstairs like a bat out of hell. But that didn't faze Jimmy. His girlfriend had a girlfriend who had a boyfriend who was a millionaire, and the boyfriend had a yacht with engines in her that were a damn sight better than anything we have in the Survey

Service. Jimmy seized that yacht at pistol point, and when the *Discovery* pulled up alongside *Alpha Draconis* we found Jimmy already there, in his spacesuit, and trying to board the ship by way of the main venturi. Had the brass completely flummoxed. They didn't know whether to give him a court-martial or a decoration."

"Unluckily," I said, "my girlfriend didn't have a girlfriend who had a boyfriend who had a yacht."

"Women," he said.

"Women," I agreed. And, Ilona, I thought.

"Here's the happy home, lad," he said.

I looked at the happy home. It wasn't any Hilton-Ritz. It was single-storied, low rambling. It was constructed of a very cheap looking plastic and was, I am correct in saying, the only shabby building I ever saw on Carinthia. It was far enough from the apron to be safe from blast hazard, but not far enough to escape fumes or noise.

"Liz knows me," said the head porter.

"Liz?"

"Used to be catering officer with I.T.C. Now she runs this joint." He shouted, raising his voice so that it drowned out the notes of the siren that, from the control tower, was giving warning of the imminent arrival of the Moon Rocket. "Liz! Liz!"

The door flew open, revealing a stout, motherly woman.

"Come in!" she yelled. "Come in, you silly things! Come in before you're choked by the smoke from that bloody five-cent firework!"

We pushed the handtruck in through the wide doorway and then, from behind the not very clean windows, watched the tumultous descent of the little ferry rocket.

"Makes more fuss about it than a big ship," said Liz disgustedly.

"When I was in the Survey Service . . ." began the head porter.

"When I was with the Interstellar Transport Commission . . ." said Liz.

When I was with Trans-Galactic Clippers, I thought.

Chapter Four

SHE WAS a good scout, was Liz Bartok.

It was just as well that she was.

The Spaceman's Hostel was nothing to write home, or anywhere else, about. Inside it was even dingier than outside. The rooms — cabins, they were called — were small, smaller even than the dogboxes comprising the officers' accommodation in an *Epsilon*-class tramp, and poorly furnished. The food, cooked by Liz, would have caused a mutiny aboard the scruffiest unit of the Rim Runner's fleet.

But the place, thanks to Liz, had its compensations.

She was a hospitable soul. As far as she was concerned I was no more and no less than a spaceman down on his luck. I was one of the family, and that was all that counted with her. I was welcome to a sip from her bottle of Slivovitz — a local liquor that tasted like rotten plums steeped in methylated spirit — any time that I cared to drop into her office. I could use the office telephone any time that I felt like it. (I tried to call Ilona several times, but got no joy from it.) I smoked her cigarettes until I had to begin a tally, to keep a record of my indebtedness.

"And what do you intend doing with yourself, Johnnie?" Liz asked me, my first evening at the Hostel.

I looked at her over my glass of plum brandy, took a sip to kill the aftertaste of the maltreated steak that had been served for dinner. "Frankly, Liz," I said, "I don't know. Of course, I'm finished as far as T.G. Clippers are concerned, and I don't suppose that your old outfit would look at me, even if I started at the bottom again as fifth mate . . ."

"Too right they wouldn't," she said bluntly. "We have our standards in the I.T.C." She grinned. "Well I suppose that they still have standards, even though I've left."

"There's always the Rim," I said. "The Terran Consul

here is also agent for Rim Runners. He tried hard to get me to sign a three-year contract."

"You could do worse," she told me. "Quite a few of our people have finished up on the Rim. There was Derek Calver. He was Chief Officer in our *Beta*-class vessels. There was Calamity Jane Arlen, who used to be one of our catering officers. Oh, quite a few. Mind you, I shouldn't care for the Rim myself. I like a sky with a few stars in it. But it's a job."

I poured some more of her plum brandy. "But I really want to stay here," I said.

She bridled. "Oh, Johnnie, this is so sudden! I know that it can't be either the cooking or the accommodation that's the attraction, so it must be me!" She laughed at my embarrassment. "It's Carinthia you mean, not the Spacemen's Hostel. But you can stay *here* as long as you like, Johnnie. It's no skin off my nose. I get paid for your board and lodging and make enough on the side to cover your drinks and smokes — and mine. Besides, I like having you here. But I'm afraid that they'll be shipping you out, soon — either back to Earth or out to the Rim." She refilled her own glass. "And what is it, or who is it, Johnnie? A woman? Is that how you missed your ship?"

"Yes." I admitted.

She chuckled. "And, of course, a Distressed Terran Spaceman isn't quite the same thing as a spaceman in a pretty uniform, simply exuding authority as a senior officer of a big ship."

"It's not like that at all," I said sharply.

"Isn't it? I'll take your word for it, Johnnie. I'll take your word for it. Yours is the one exception that proves the rule."

"All right," I said. "I'm a bloody fool, Liz. But it's the way I'm made. It boils down to this: I can't help feeling that if I'm able to make a go of things on this planet, if I'm able to establish myself, I stand a chance."

"Johnnie," she told me seriously, "please face facts. Your background's all wrong, your training. Spacemen just can't make a go of things ashore except in the very few jobs for which they're qualified. And you'll never get a post on the Port Captain's staff or as a stevedore supervisor here, on Carinthia. Everybody knows that you're the ex-second mate of *Lightning*, who missed his ship. You already have a reputation for unreliability."

"But there must be something," I said.

"Digging ditches, Johnnie? Shovelling sludge in the sewage conversion plant? Tallying cargo here at the spaceport? And that doesn't pay as well as the manual jobs . . ."

"But there must be something," I insisted.

"There's not," she said firmly. "There's not, my dear. You'd better sign that contract and ship out to the Rim."

She was wrong — although, after four days of fruitless job hunting, I was ready to admit that she was right. On the fifth morning I was reading the *New Prague Advertiser*, turning first of all to the classified ads, the *Situations Vacant* columns. Housewives' Help, I noted, still advertised for salesmen. They might, I thought bitterly, have given me a trial, in spite of the adverse result of their psychological tests. "Frankly, Mr Petersen," the Personnel Manager had told me, "you couldn't sell a steak to a starving man, let alone an Automaid Mark VII to a lady who's quite satisfied with her old Automaid Mark VI."

Then, near the bottom of the column, I saw something that just might be promising: *Young men wanted. Interesting, adventurous, well-paid employment. Apply Stefan Vynalek, Heinlein's Building, Masaryk Square*.

I took the paper through to the kitchen, showed it to Liz. She left our breakfast eggs to vulcanize in the pan (she maintained that she had become sick and tired of automatic galley equipment during her years in space and also maintained, with considerable truth, that no machine could bring the personal touch to cooking) and read the ad.

She said, "I knew a Steve Vynalek once, Johnnie. Quite

a boy, he was. A pity that this isn't the same one. I could recommend you to him."

"Thanks, Liz. Of course, it might be the same one."

"It couldn't be. The one I knew was a detective inspector. And policemen are as bad as spacemen: when they retire or resign or get fired all that they're good for is watchmen's jobs." She sniffed loudly, turned abruptly, glared at the ruined eggs. She threw the contents of the pan into the disposal chute, remarking, "It's a good job that Imperial Earth is paying the bills in this dump."

"I think that I'll apply," I said.

"Do just that. But have your breakfast first. Disappointment's bad on an empty stomach."

After breakfast she called me into her office. She said, "It's just possible that it might be the Steve I know. I'll ring and find out."

She found Vynalek's number in the directory — it was listed under Stefan Vynalek, Incorporated — pushed buttons for the combination. A severely efficient, but attractive blonde looked out of the little screen. "S.V.," she said briefly.

"May I speak with Mr Vynalek?" asked Liz.

"May I ask your business, Madam? I assure you that I am competent to deal with all routine inquiries."

Liz turned to grin at me, then returned her attention to the phone. "Please tell Mr Vynalek," she said, "that this call is in connection with the *Beta Carinae* smuggling case."

"Will you hold the line, Madam?" asked the girl coldly.

"Beta Carinae?" I said.

"Yes, Johnnie. The famous smuggling case was when I first met Steve. He and his ham-handed pals just about took the ship apart hunting for that illegal consignment of euphorine. That was when I first met him. If this Stefan Vynalek is *my* Steve, he'll remember all right."

"Liz!" came a voice from the phone. "Long time no see."

"Long time no see you, Steve. Were you interested in

me only when I was a member of the criminal classes?"

"I'm always interested in you, Liz."

And I was interested in him. The screen displayed the face of a man no longer young, but far from old. Grizzled hair topped a face that, in spite of the darkness of the skin and the deeper darkness along the jowls, was boyishly smooth. The black eyes were lively, yet penetrating.

"And did the cops fire you, Steve? Did they find you out at last?"

"I resigned."

"That's an answer to only the first question."

He laughed. "It will have to do."

"And are you in the smuggling business now?"

"Nothing so romantic, Liz. I've set up shop as a private eye. The connections help. I was able to get a licence for all the apparatus I needed."

"And would a spaceman be able to work this apparatus?"

"What do you mean, Liz?"

I saw your ad in the morning rag."

"Are you applying? But I was advertising for young men, not young women."

"Oh, all right, all right. I'm a poor, old grounded spacewoman. But I have a spaceman here who's tired of doing nothing."

"John Petersen," he said. "Late second officer of the Trans-Galactic Clipper *Lightning*. Missed his ship. Stranded on Carinthia until such time as the Terran Consul can arrange his passage —"

I moved so that I was within the scope of the scanner. I asked, "How did you know, Mr Vynalek?"

He grinned. "I have my methods, Watson." Then: "Everybody in New Prague knew that *Lightning* made a late blast-off. The reason for this was published in the rags. And there's only one place where a Distressed Spaceman will be staying." He paused, studying my face. "I'll promise nothing, John. I'll promise nothing. But there might just be a place for you in my organization."

"Thanks, Mr Vynalek," I said. "But the only apparatus I can handle is navigational apparatus. Your spy beams and analysers and reconstructors —"

"You've been reading too many detective stories," he said. "The wrong period, at that." He turned to Liz. "Come out tonight, Liz, and bring John with you. I may be able to take him off your hands."

Chapter Five

THIS, I thought, as I walked with Liz the short distance from the subway station to Heinlein's Building, will be my third business appointment in Masaryk Square. My first was with Maleter, the second was with the Consul. And this one? Third time lucky?

"Steve must be doing well," said Liz.

"Why?" I asked rather stupidly.

"Rents are high in the Square, especially for space in the more modern buildings, such as this one. They're high enough for a one-room office. Office and apartment combined must cost a fortune."

"And they say," I remarked, "that crime doesn't pay."

"Not half it doesn't," she said.

We passed through the revolving doors into the hallway of the building — plain it was, severe, almost, but fabric and masonry were quietly opulent, had been imported from a score of worlds — and looked at the names of the tenants listed on the directory board. Stefan Vynalek, it seemed, occupied the entire top floor. Transport to the upper levels was provided by lift shafts, or, if you're using them to go down, drop shafts. Liz beamed. "If I ever get round to owning a sky-scraper," she said, "I'll have these installed instead of those old-fashioned elevators. They always remind me of free falls." We rode the cushion of compressed air to the top of the shaft, stepped out into a short corridor. At the end of it was a plain grey door, and on the door, in plain black lettering: STEFAN VYNALEK, INCORPORATED.

The door opened and Vynalek stood there.

I was a little surprised; somehow I had assumed that he would be a tall, big man. (The head-and-shoulders picture presented by a telephone screen is often misleading.) But, I thought, amusing myself with the analogy, a successful detective will be a ferret rather than a lion. Not that there was anything of the ferret about Vynalek — outwardly, at least. If one insisted on zoological comparisons, he was like a small, agile, infinitely shrewd hunting cat.

"Liz!" he said, stepping forward to embrace her briefly.

"Steve!" She disengaged herself. "This is John."

He shook hands. "Good to know you, John. But don't stand out here, getting the premises a bad name. Come in."

We followed him through a severely functional outer office, through an inner one that was almost as plain. Beyond that was the living room of his apartment. It, too, was functional; and its function was comfort. It reminded me of a small public room aboard a luxurious modern ship. The window that occupied all of one wall could well have been one of the viewscreens that are becoming standard fittings in the better class spacecraft — the make-believe windows that, in the depths of space, present the illusion of planetary scenery. This actual window looked out over the city, over the vast complexity of lights, static and in motion, beyond the urban illuminations, out to the vivid streaks of incandescence in the black sky that marked the descent of an interplanetary freighter, inbound from Silesia, the mining planet next out in orbit from Carinthia's sun.

"A god's-eye view, Steve," said Liz.

He laughed. "Or a cop's-eye view. Drinks? Slivovitz?

Lager?"

He poured plum brandy for Liz and himself, lager for me. While I sipped it I began to indulge my curiosity.

"You seem to possess your share of detective instincts," said our host.

"Sorry, Steve," I apologized. "I'm afraid it's a bad habit of mine. I always look at people's bookshelves. Very often I get a fair idea of what they're like from their reading matter."

"I always do the same, John," he told me. "Now, as you have already observed, I own a fine collection of detective fiction, none of it modern, all of it from the vintage period. You'll find all the twentieth-century masters here: Conan Doyle, Chesterton, Macdonald, Raymond Chandler, Agatha Christie. . . ."

"And the rest," said Liz. "I can see that your tastes haven't changed. I remember how excited you were when you were searching *Beta Carinae* for contraband and you found an ancient, tattered reprint of some old book by some old author called Spillane. But what you, a professional detective, can see in this rubbish. . . ."

"It's not rubbish," he said quietly. "It's good, sound stuff. And, as a matter of fact, it was these very books that encouraged me to resign from the force and to set up shop on my own account." He was warming to his theme. "The trouble with every modern police department is that it's too obsessed with gadgetry. If a crime can't be solved by electronic means, then it's insoluble. And you'd be surprised, and shocked, at how many insoluble crimes there are. Now, if you'll come through to the laboratory. I'll show you what the modern detective is up against."

He took us from his sitting room, into a compartment which at first glance, was like the control room of a spaceship. The walls were covered with switchboards and control panels. In the centre of the floor was something that looked like a chart tank, a spherical transparency all of five feet in diameter.

He flicked a switch on the pedestal and the globe came

alive. It was like looking into a queer, three-dimensional mirror. In it we saw the globe, with ourselves standing around it, and in the pictured globe we saw another pictured globe, and in that. . . .

"Don't try to count," he warned. "One of our spy beam operators at headquarters did just that, turning up the magnification all the time, and it took the headquarters psychiatrist all of six months to get him straightened out again."

"So this is the spy beam," I said.

"This is the spy beam." He stooped to the controls. "Going down."

We went down.

We pried into the two apartments that occupied the floor below ours. We stood, figuratively, behind the armchair of the woman who was reading a novel. Steve adjusted angle and magnification until we were able to read it with her: *urgent, upthrusting. And she, warmly receptive, hotly longing, yet shuddering from the touch of him, shuddering from but, ambivalently, surging to, her arms and the steel-strong slenderness of her thighs capturing and holding, her.* . . .

She turned the page.

"Blast her," swore Liz. "It was just getting interesting."

"A few minor adjustments," said Steve, "and you can still read it."

"Oh, skip it. Just find out the title and the author, will you?"

"Can do."

The angle of vision changed. Liz said. "*Lalage*, by Dupless. I must remember that."

Under Steve's control the spy beam hunted, now and again pausing briefly.

"No, Steve!" cried Liz. "Move on, damn you. This isn't decent."

"A pretty girl having a shower? This is cleaner than the pornography that you were wallowing in."

"Move on," she said.

The spy beam moved on. Through deserted offices it ranged, and through offices in which overtime was being worked. In Carinthian Iron and Steel a disgruntled looking clerk was speaking into the telephone, making notes on a pad as he did so. We could see the face and shoulders of a uniformed spaceman in the screen, could hear his voice. "Yes, I know damn well that we were late berthing. But that's no excuse for not having the mail down." In Lolita Fashions a plump, effeminate man was pinning swathes of glowing material about the slim body of a bored model. Liz sighed, then said, "Wait awhile, Steve, there's no hurry." Steve snapped, "If I pry into trade secrets I'm liable to lose my licence." We walked, figuratively, with the spy beam along a corridor, came to a door behind the frosted glass of which shone a light, a door bearing the legend: LONGSHOREMAN'S UNION.

"More overtime," I said. "I suppose that they'll be arranging gangs for that ore carrier that's just in from Silesia."

"Could be," said Steve. "Could be. Let's find out, shall we?"

And then it was like coming up against a brick wall. There was an opacity that we could not, from any angle of approach, penetrate.

"There," said Steve. "You see. Or you don't see. It amounts to the same thing. To every weapon there is a defensive. The criminal classes have their own scientists and technicians."

"But surely this, this defence is illegal?"

"The use of a spy beam is barely legal, even by the police department. Without influential friends, I, as a private individual, could never have gotten a licence to own and operate this one. And the monitor at headquarters will have registered the fact that this one is being used right now. But the use of a blocker is absolutely legal. Anybody may use any means whatsoever to protect his own privacy."

"Then I'm surprised that more people don't have

blockers installed."

"First, they're very expensive. Secondly, not everybody has anything to hide from the law."

"That girl in the shower had plenty," said Liz.

"It would have been a shame to have hidden it," I said.

"Men!" she said disgustedly.

"This would be a handy piece of navigational equipment," I said, changing the subject. "In many ways it would be better than radar for approach and landing."

"Yes," said Liz. "Wouldn't it? I can just see all the lecherous spacehounds in the control room peering into blondes' bathrooms instead of watching a nice, clear picture of the landing field."

"What's the effective range?" I asked.

"Anywhere on Carinthia, on either hemisphere. And out as far as the Moon."

"The Moon?"

He grinned. "Yes. The Moon."

"Wenceslaus, you mean."

"The Moon, I mean. That's the trouble with you Earthmen — there's only one Moon with an upper-case *M*, and that's Luna. As far as we're concerned, there's only one Moon with an upper-case *M*, and that's Wenceslaus often enough, but I've never been there."

I said, "I've passed Wenceslaus often enough, but I've never been there."

"Feel like a trip?"

"To Wenceslaus?" I laughed. "Oh, you mean by spy beam."

"That isn't what I meant, John, but we can do just that. Now."

"Must you?" asked Liz. "After I left I.T.C. I was a few months in the Moon Rockets and saw enough of that damned dust ball to last me a lifetime."

"Then you can amuse yourself in the kitchen," said Steve. "Coffee and sandwiches would be welcome."

"I could cook us a proper supper," she said wistfully.

Steve shuddered slightly. "I couldn't impose on you,

Liz. Just coffee and sandwiches will be fine."

"Toasted sandwiches?"

"Yes," he said reluctantly.

"If you'll show me where things live," she said.

"All right. Are you coming through, John, or staying here?"

"If you don't mind," I said, "I'd like to play with this thing."

"As you please. The controls are quite simple. And you may as well get some practice in its use, not that I think you will be using it."

"So I haven't made the grade, Steve?"

He smiled warmly. "I neither said nor implied that, John."

Chapter Six

I STILL FEEL ashamed of what I did as soon as I was alone, and yet I am sure that most men in my circumstances would have done the same. The temptation was strong, and I was not strong enough to resist the temptation.

The controls of the spy beam were simple. Turning one of the knobs controlled apparent altitude. I brought the picture up from the floor upon which the Longshoremen's Union was situated, up to the level of Stefan Vynalek's apartment, then to and above the roof level. I was looking down on to the Square, to the fountains with their rainbow floodlighting around the symbolic statuary in the centre, to the rank of stone spaceships with the houseflags of the companies limned in coloured light.

When I had come ashore from *Lightning* that night, the air taxi had carried me over the Square. So, obviously, my destination had been on an extension of a line drawn from the spaceport to the Square. Fingers clumsy at first on the controls, I hunted along that line, looking for a big advertising sign that I had seen on our starboard hand, a great, tilted bottle from which a glowing, golden stream poured into an outheld glass. I found the sign at last, realizing that the taxi driver must have made a slight detour so as to treat his customer to a view of the centre of the city.

Then, a little further on, there had been the floodlit towers of the university, and beyond them the darkness of the park, and, beyond that, the tall apartment houses. It was like piloting an atmosphere flier — an incredibly silent machine with incredibly sensitive controls. I skimmed over the park, slowed as I approached the dimly glowing columns of the apartment houses.

Outside Greengates I hesitated, then lifted my viewpoint up the face of the building, past the row after row of windows and balconies, past the expanse of mirrorlike glass that, with their one-way vision, protected the privacy of those behind them.

The top floor, I thought. The top floor. . . .

"You might as well save yourself the trouble, John," said Steve sympathetically.

I started, jumping back from the controls as though they had suddenly become red-hot.

"But go on," he said. "You've come so far. It would be a shame to give up now. Go on."

"I — I'm not sure that I want to."

"Go on," he said again, a faint yet unmistakable crackle of authority in his voice.

After a few minutes of futile manipulation of the controls I stood up. "A blocker," I said.

"Yes, a blocker. Perhaps it's just as well for your peace of mind that there is one."

"But, she's not a criminal."

"How do you know?" He smiled tiredly. "She's not, as a matter of fact. But there are certain activities for which privacy is desirable. Look at it this way. Just try to imagine a rich, influential woman, a woman who has reason to suspect that her husband's late nights out with the boys are not entirely innocent. Just suppose that this woman knows somebody highly placed in police headquarters, somebody with access to a spy beam. And just suppose that her husband is among those who have contributed towards the expense of the installation of a blocker in a certain lady's apartment. . . ."

"You're supposing one hell of a lot," I said.

"I know one hell of a lot," he told me.

"You must find it hard to live with yourself," I said.

"At times I do. John. At times I do."

He put the bottles and glasses that he was carrying down on a bench, asked, "More lager?"

"I'd prefer something stronger."

"I thought you would." He poured two glasses of Slivovitz. "Here's to crime. Talking of crime, I'm afraid that that's just what's going on in the kitchen. Liz is a great person, but as a cook. . . ."

"I know."

He said, "I'm rather sorry that I want you, John. My advice to you would be to get off this planet as soon as possible. But, as I said, I want you."

"I'm glad that somebody does," I said.

He said, "But I have to be sure before I hire you. After all, this is a job in which a certain amount of integrity is desirable. Putting it bluntly, you let down Trans-Galactic Clippers. How can I be sure that you won't let down Stefan Vynalek, Incorporated?"

"How can you be sure that anybody won't let anybody down?" I asked bitterly.

"How, indeed? But if you tell me your story, John, I shall be able to make my judgement. Unless I know all the facts of the case I shan't be able to."

I held out my glass for a refill. "All right. As you know, I was second officer of *Lightning*. Ilona was one of the passengers. She was at my table. We clicked from the very start. She insisted that I visit her in her apartment the one night that *Lightning* was in port. We . . . overslept. I missed the ship. That's all."

"That was all?"

I hesitated. "No. There's more. There was a drug, euphorine. . . ."

"Euphorine," he said softly. "Infinite pleasure, infinitely prolonged. And you both took it?"

"Yes."

"It's funny stuff," he said briskly. "As you know, it's no longer illegal, but it's still damned expensive. There are people who think that it's worth paying for. There are people who think that an affair should end not with a whimper, but a bang. As you know, great emotional stress can cause personality changes. It is not so well known that pleasurable emotions, almost unendurably intensified, can have a similar effect. Your Ilona, if it's any consolation to you, was acting as kindly as she knew how to. She was giving you one last, big night, after which the slate would be wiped clean, leaving both of you free to return to your normal lives without regret."

"But she took an antidote."

"She did? Tell me, just what did happen?"

I told him, omitting nothing. He listened in silence, thoughtfully refilling my glass when I paused to take breath.

"An ungodly mixture," he said when I was finished. "Euphorine tends to deteriorate with age, its effects becoming somewhat unpredictable. The stuff that both of you swallowed must have been several months old. Added to the unpredictability of the drug you have the unpredictability of the female mind. But I think I can work out what happened, and you may feel a little better when I've told you."

"Go on," I said.

"The antidote," he told me, "is used by those who want to have their cake *and* eat it. The euphorine gives them the big night, all in glorious Technicolor, and then the antidote cancels the aftereffects.

"But try to look at things from Ilona's viewpoint. She wakes up, and finds that even though there's no longer any mad passion there's no allergy. Furthermore, there's a strong feeling of responsibility. You've missed your ship, and the fault, partly, at least, is hers. She thinks to herself, All right, if I have to keep this bum I may as well love him again. So she takes the antidote, but it's deteriorated, or she's been off the stuff for so long that it doesn't have the right effect. She feels now, as she should have felt as a result of the euphorine. Do you follow?"

"I — I think so."

"Good. Now, if you don't mind, tell me what your feelings are. I'm not prying, but I spent a long time on the Narcotics Squad and I picked up a deal of knowledge about the effects of various drugs. I may be able to help."

"My feelings? Oh, there's a numbness. And a loneliness. I want her badly, but not the way that a man should want a woman. That blasted stuff has killed something."

"A typical reaction," he said briskly. "A typical reaction, that is, to overage euphorine. But it will wear off."

"I hope so. But what I find really sickening, now that you've told me what must have happened, is the strong element of chance, malign chance, in it all. If the euphorine hadn't been overage; if we hadn't played around with it, anyhow; if our reactions had been according to the book; if the antidote had worked as it should have done. . . ."

"If you could put the clock back," he added, grinning.

"If I could put the clock back," I agreed.

He sniffed audibly, saying, "I smell burning. Liz insisted on making toasted sandwiches. Supper will be ready soon. She'll probably bring it in here." He raised his voice. "Now, Wenceslaus, the moon of Carinthia. . . ."

His skilled fingers played over the spy ray controls. In the transparent sphere of the viewer New Prague fell down and away, dwindled to a spot of luminosity, one of many, on the night side of the planet. The viewpoint abruptly changed and a gleaming crescent rushed towards us — a crescent that suddenly was a globe with a sliver of its surface brilliantly sunlit. And that sliver, with almost frightening rapidity, became a great, gleaming plain, a plain upon whose featureless surface the cities rode like ships.

"You know," said Liz, setting down the supper tray with a clatter on the bench, "I'd prefer seeing blondes having a bath to this."

"You needn't look," said Steve.

We hovered briefly over one of the cities, over the great, shallow dome broken by odd-looking minarets and cupolas. We skimmed over the dust sea towards the terminator, towards another, much smaller dome. Our viewpoint dropped rapidly down to the expanse of gleaming metal — dropped and stopped.

"Another blocker," I said cleverly.

"Another blocker," agreed Steve.

"And what master criminal lives on Wenceslaus?" I asked.

"No master criminal would live on Wenceslaus," said Liz, "unless he was doing time in the penal colony there."

"You're biased," Steve told her. "As a matter of fact, though, that place doesn't belong to a master criminal. It belongs to a rich man, a very rich man. Fergus is his name."

"Fergus? There was a Fergus in T.G. Clippers — interstellar drive chief engineer. He made a series of fantastically lucky investments, made a fortune and retired."

"That's the man," said Steve.

Chapter Seven

WHEN WE LEFT his apartment, Steve gave me a half-dozen of his precious books to read. "Bring them back tomorrow evening," he told me. "And then we'll talk."

I hefted the bundle in my hand. "How did you know that I'd mastered the quick reading technique?" I asked.

He grinned. "Elementary, my dear Watson. People who have to study to pass examinations become quick readers. Spacemen have to study to pass examinations. So. . . ."

"You win," I said.

"Good. Tomorrow night, then. Goodnight, Liz. And thanks for coming out."

"Thank you for asking us," she said. "You must come out to the Hostel sometime, Steve, for a real meal. I can do much better in my own kitchen."

"I'm sure that you can," he agreed politely.

On our way to the station, Liz said, "You're in. He likes you, and he can use you. But I'm inclined to think that you might be better off out on the Rim."

"How do you know?"

"Oh, I know Steve. And we had quite a long talk while I was out in the kitchen fixing supper. He as good as said that even if you were a complete drongo he'd still want you, just because you're a spaceman."

"Nice to know that my qualifications are of some value elsewhere than on the Rim," I said.

"But I still don't think that you should accept Steve's offer."

"Why not? I thought that he was a friend of yours."

"Was and is. But he's a policeman. He's still a policeman, even though he's in private practice. Policemen look at things different from other people, just as, I suppose, we look at things differently from planetlubbers. He's a policeman, which means that he's ruthless when he has to be, and when he doesn't have to be. He'll not care how

38

many corns he tramples on as long as he brings a case to a successful conclusion."

"Most policemen," I said, "carefully avoid trampling on corns if the owners of said corns are good for a backhander."

"Steve," she said, "was never like that. That's one reason why he left the force."

We boarded the capsule, sped through the pneumatic tube to the spaceport station, making desultory conversation. We walked across the floodlit apron, skirting the area of activity around the big ore carrier, to the Hostel. I wondered if the boys had got their mail yet, but most of them, apart from the duty officer and engineer, would be home by now and not worrying about a few letters. Lucky bastards, I thought, with homes to go to, and with a ship to live aboard if they had no homes ashore.

Liz said, "I suppose you'll be putting in a night's heavy reading."

"I may as well get started on these now."

"All right. You get turned in and I'll make some coffee. I'll bring it in to you."

I was in my cot, making a start on the first of the books, when she came in. She was carrying a vacuum jug, a cup and a pack of cigarettes.

"Thanks, Liz," I said.

She said, "I'm pleased to be able to do something for you, Johnnie. I wish I could do more."

I looked at her. She was wearing a wrap, an almost transparent garment, and it was obvious that she was wearing nothing underneath it. Her figure, I realized suddenly, was good. Her face was lined, but there are some faces that are made beautiful by the lines of experience, and hers was one of them. I wondered how I had ever got the impression that she was middle-aged and motherly. Motherly, yes, but most men want a mother as well as a mistress.

She put the coffee and the other things down on the bedside table, sat on the bed. I could feel the nearness of her — and it did nothing to me. But, perhaps . . . I put my arm around her and she did not resist. I kissed her.

I said, "I'm sorry, Liz, but it's no good."

"I can tell that," she whispered tonelessly. "I can tell that. Oh, Johnnie, Johnnie, the only way that you'll ever get that woman out of your system is by sleeping with another woman."

"I know. But —"

"But you can't," she said briskly, getting to her feet. "Never mind, it will come. Meanwhile, coffee, cigarettes. I can't give you any more."

"I'm sorry that you can't," I told her.

"So am I," she agreed.

She left me, and I was genuinely sorry to see her go. She left me, and I turned to the books for company. They were fascinating stuff, some of them better than others. In some of them the private eye solved his cases by intensive brainwork while the police stood around in admiration; in others the private eye blundered around like a bull in a china shop, guzzling whisky and seducing blondes, getting beaten up between times by both cops and crooks, and still solved his cases. What it was all suposed to prove I didn't know, but I read on.

It was very late when I put the light out and, the following morning, Liz let me sleep on. It was a little before noon when she awakened me. She said, "I'm sorry, Johnnie, but you're wanted on the phone."

"All right," I said.

I fell rather than jumped out of bed, slipped into a robe, went through to the office. I saw the plump face of the Terran Consul peering out from the little screen. As soon as I was within the scope of the scanner he spoke.

"Ah, good morning. Mr Petersen. Or should I say good afternoon? But no matter."

"Good morning, sir."

"Your, ah, contract."

"Contract?"

"With the Rim Runners. Have you decided to sign it

yet?"

"No. But I'll not be signing."

The Consul cleared his throat. "I called this morning to give you good news. The Sundowner Line's *Waltzing Matilda*, from Nova Caledon to Faraway via Elsinore, has been diverted to Carinthia. I can arrange a passage for you in her to the Rim Worlds. *If* you sign the contract."

"I told you. I'm not signing."

"Then, Mr Petersen, as agent for the Rim Government I wash my hands of you."

"And as Terran Consul?"

"I shall, unfortunately, be responsible for you until you are shipped out in *Delta Eridani*."

"Back to Earth?"

"Where else?"

"And suppose I don't want to leave Carinthia?"

"Then, as Terran Consul, I shall wash my hands of you. Imperial Earth will no longer be responsible for your keep at the Hostel. Your deportation will be handled — expeditiously, no doubt — by the local authorities."

"And suppose I've found a job?"

He laughed sneeringly. "Spacemen, my man, are unemployed on any planetary surface."

"Goodbye," I said switching off.

Liz, who had been present, said, "You're very sure of yourself, Johnnie."

"Am I?"

"I still think that you should have taken the offer. On the Rim you'd be making a fresh start."

"I'll be making a fresh start here."

"No, Johnnie. It won't be a fresh start. You're just staying on so that you can, you hope, restart something that's finished, irrevocably finished."

"What's been finished," I said, "can be restarted."

"But it can't. Damn it all, even though I haven't been eaves-dropping I've known every time you've tried to put a call through to that bitch, every time that you've been given the brush-off."

"She's not a bitch," I said sharply. "And as for what happened that night, we were both of us unlucky. There was an unfortunate combination of circumstances."

"Unfortunate," she said, "for you."

"Oh, skip it, Liz. As they say on Nova Caledon, I must dree my own weird."

"All right." She put on an artificial brightness of manner. "Breakfast? Or will it be lunch."

"As long as it's food," I said. "But I'll tell you what I should like: a couple of those good, crusty rolls and some cheese."

"But I like cooking," she said rather pathetically.

"All right, then we'll have something cooked."

It was the least that I could do for her, and I wished, most sincerely, that I could have done more.

Chapter Eight

THAT NIGHT, as arranged, I went out again to Steve's apartment.

He took the books from me as soon as I was inside his door, lost no time in returning them to their places on the shelves. He waited, however, until I was seated, a tall glass in my hands, before questioning me.

"Well, John, and what did you think of them?"

"Readable, Steve, very readable. And they do, in a rather warped sort of way, give a picture of those times, although it's hard to realize that while those quite impossible characters were boozing, wenching and beating each other up, the Space Age was just beginning."

He said, "You have a certain bias, John. And, after all, detective thrillers weren't the only popular literature in the twentieth-century. A friend of mine, for example, has a really fine collection of twentieth-century science-fiction. There's plenty about the Space Age in that. There are plenty of remarkably accurate guesses — and even more away to hell and gone off the beam."

"But those writers were lucky," I said. "About the only thing that the modern science-fiction writer has to write about is time travel."

"Those old-timers wrote about it too. But we're not talking about science-fiction. We're talking about whodunnits. What would you say is the essential message of these books?"

"They're not the sort of stuff that one reads for a message. They never were."

"Go on," he told me. "Think. Use Hercule Poirot's 'little grey cells.' "

I thought.

I voiced my thoughts hesitantly.

"The message, if you can call it that, seems to be this. The message seems to be that the machinery of organized crime-prevention and -detection is too cumbersome. The message seems to be that one resourceful man can achieve more than a big and well-equipped police force. And there's another angle. Very often this one, resourceful man — or not so resourceful — having blundered into the middle of some sort of mess acts as a catalyst so that the whole lot blows up, very often right in his face."

"Good. In other words, the private operator, without apparatus, often does better than the police, with apparatus. And those stories were written before the police possessed much in the way of apparatus, before they became slaves to their own electronic gadgetry."

"That's about it, Steve."

He went on, "As you have already seen, I do have some apparatus. Spy beam, analyser, all the rest of it. You have seen the spy beam in operation. You have seen how it can be countered."

"Yes."

"Well the problem is to get a man inside one of those places using a blocker."

"The Longshoremen's Union office?"

"No. And not the top floor apartment of Greengates, either." He grinned a little maliciously. "You remember when I turned the beam on to the Moon?"

"Yes."

"And you remember the Fergus place?"

"Of course."

"That's where I want to get you, John."

"Why me?"

"The Moon," he explained patiently, "is airless. None of my operatives here on Carinthia knows the first thing about the problems of working in a spacesuit. I did have to wear a suit once, when I was still on the force, and the experience almost killed me. Some psychological deficency or other."

"You could have recruited an operative from the Moon Colony," I said.

"I tried that. But everybody in the Colony works, and everybody is too well-paid to consider taking additional employment."

"There must be people here on Carinthia — tourists, people who've been to the Moon on pleasure or business."

"People," he said, "who, on the rare occasions that they were out of the pressurized cities, were skimming over the surface in the pressurized cabins of dustsleds. Mind you, you might do nothing more than that yourself. But there's always the chance that you may have to do some footslogging outside."

"Then how am I to get into the Fergus place?"

"That's up to you."

"Illegal entry?"

"Private eyes," he said, "sometimes have to bend the law a little."

"Is this Fergus bending the law himself? Or breaking it?"

"Not that I know of."

"Then what's all this about?"

"The government," he said, "is curious. The government would like to satisfy its curiosity. The government has heard rumours that Mr Fergus has invented something — something that may well change the course of history."

"Most inventions do that," I said.

"Yes," he agreed. "They do. But they do it after they've been invented, not before."

"What do you mean?"

"What I said. Look at it this way. Suppose you could go back, armed with all the necessary knowledge, to take charge of the control room of the Skoda Power Station an hour or so before the piles started to go critical. You'd be instrumental in saving thousands of lives."

"I saw the explosion," I said, "from a million miles out. I was fourth mate of the old *Taiping* at the time. We were coming in when it happened."

"And if that explosion could be stopped. . . ."

"But it couldn't be, Steve. That would mean time travel, and time travel is nothing but fantasy."

"I used to think the same, once," he said soberly. "But Central Intelligence is almost convinced that this man Fergus has some sort of time travel. Central Intelligence has sold the idea to the President. The President, who is already famous for his humanitarian principles, thinks that time travel could be used to expunge disasters like the Skoda affair from the pages of history."

"But how do they know? What do they know?"

"Not much. There was a disgruntled laboratory technician whom Fergus fired — he'd been making passes at the old man's daughter — and he sang. He did his singing, eventually, in front of an analyser. There wasn't much to it, but there was enough to get the Intelligence boys to thinking."

"Then why doesn't Central Intelligence carry out its own investigation?"

"Because Central Intelligence is in the same rut as the

police. It's got a skyscraper full of apparatus like a mad scientist's nightmare, but it can't crack the shell that the real mad scientist, who's determined to work in secrecy, has built about himself."

"With all due respect, Steve, why did they come to you, a private eye?"

"Because when I was on the force, I made no secret of my views on superscientific detection. And I solved quite a few cases without the aid of electronic gadgetry."

"It makes sense of a sort," I grudgingly admitted.

"It makes sense," he stated flatly. "No, John, it's your turn to talk. We'll see if you make sense."

"What shall I talk about?"

"This time travel business. Fergus, as you know, was once chief engineer with your old outfit. Does that make any sort of sense?"

"Could do," I admitted. "Could do. He was interstellar drive chief engineer. That means that he was in full charge of the Mannschenn Drive Unit, responsible for the maintenance of the Carlotti Beacon equipment."

"The Carlotti Beacons? Aren't they those weird affairs like Mobius Strips coiled around attenuated Klein Flasks out at the spaceport?"

"That's as good a description as any. Well, as you know, interstellar travel *is* time travel of a sort. We have a faster-than-light drive, but we get it by cheating. Putting it very crudely, an interstellar ship goes ahead in space and astern in time."

"Then there *is* time travel."

"No. There are limitations. If there were no limitations we should have instantaneous transit between the stars, and the intergalactic drive would be more than a science-fictioneer's dream."

"But these Carlotti Beacons — As I understand it, there is no time lag between the transmission and reception of a signal from and to anywhere in the galaxy."

"But that does not involve the transmission of matter."

"You're the expert," he grinned. "But this Fergus —

he's an expert too."

"It's a well-known fact," I told him, "that people who work all their lives in the time-twisting fields of the drive are more than a little mad."

"Which," he said, "brings us back to the concept of the mad scientist. All right, Fergus is mad. But what about the odd stories one hears — the Rim Ghosts, and the ships that vanish? What about *Beta Orionis?* Her loss has never been accounted for, has it?"

"Ships have always vanished," I said, "ever since there have been ships — surface ships, subsurface ships, spaceships. What you might call an occupational hazard."

"In the case of interstellar ships," he insisted, "some sort of a fault in time would account for the disappearances very neatly."

I laughed. "I almost believe that you believe in this crazy time travel idea yourself."

"I almost do believe in it. After all, the Central Intelligence boys are no fools. They may rely too heavily on their gadgets, but those same gadgets are the very latest, and their operators are extremely well trained." He got to his feet. "I have the recording here of that lab technician's interrogation. As I told you, they put it through the analyser, and the analyser indicated that he was speaking the truth. Just wait a couple of seconds while I get it, then I'll play it back to you."

Chapter Nine

WHEN SOMETHING has been repeated enough times you remember it well. I can remember, word for word, that interrogation:

Q. Your name is Igor Kravenko?

A. That is correct.

Q. You are a laboratory technician?

A. That is correct.

Q. You were employed by Dr Fergus as an assistant to him in his laboratory on the Moon?

A. By *Mister* Fergus. He can claim no academic titles.

Q. But Mr Fergus does possess qualifications. Can you tell us their nature?

A. Yes. The old bastard made no secret of them. Extra first-class engineer. Mannschenn Drive, with Carlotti Beacon Maintenance Endorsement.

Q. And your qualifications, Mr Kravenko?

A. Bachelor of Veterinary Science, University of New Prague.

Q. Veterinary Science? No degree in physics? No training in physics?

A. No.

Q. What were your duties in the Fergus laboratory?

A. I was in charge of the livestock.

Q. So Mr Fergus was engaged in biological experiments?

A. No.

Q. Are you sure of that?

A. No.

Q. Please make up your mind, Mr Kravenko.

A. I was only a small boy around the place. He told me nothing. All that I had to do was to keep the mountain cats in good order.

Q. The mountain cats. . . . We are all of us familiar with these animals, but perhaps you, as a trained veterinarian, can give us further information about them and their habits that may prove of value.

A. What information can I give? They're quadrupeds, quasi-mamalian, omnivorous . . . .

Q. Anything else?

A. They hibernate.

Q. And these mountain cats in the Moon laboratory — were they in a state of hibernation?

48

A. Some of them.

Q. What do you mean by "some of them?"

A. Roughly half of them.

Q. Roughly half?

A. They were shipped up from Carinthia in equal numbers from the summer and the winter hemisphere. Then, owing to the experiments, there was a certain confusion.

Q. A certain confusion?

A. Yes. There was artificially-induced hibernation. There was artificially-induced awakening.

Q. How? Drugs? Diet? Variations in temperature?

A. All three, I think.

Q. You think? Did you take no part in these experiments?

A. No. I was just the animal keeper. It was my job to see that the non-hibernating mountain cats were maintained in conditions — diet, temperature and all the rest of it — approximating as closely as possible to those of their natural habitat in summer. With the hibernating ones it was much easier — merely temperature control.

Q. And the experiments were performed on both groups of mountain cats?

A. Yes.

Q. Can you describe the experiments?

A. I — I found it all very confusing.

Q. Can you be more explicit?

A. He, Fergus, would do something, and I would have the feeling that I'd seen him do it before, but not quite the same way.

Q. Can you give an example?

A. He'd put a sleeping mountain cat, a hibernating mountain cat, in the field of his apparatus, and all that would happen would be that it would go into an even deeper sleep, a sleep from which it was quite impossible to awaken it by any means. Or it might be a lively mountain cat and it would at once go into that unnatural deep sleep.

Q. But you seem to be describing no more than experiments in artificially-induced hibernation.

A. No. No, there was more to it than that.

Q. What do you mean?

A. It was all so confused.

Q. Please try to be more explicit.

A. I'm trying to be. But it was all . . . confusing. As you know, they're prettily marked, these mountain cats. Very distinctive markings, some of them. There's one I remember. It was black, with a distinct white cross on its left side. It was one of the hibernating ones. We put it in the field of the apparatus. It woke up suddenly, with a healthy appetite, with normal reactions. Two days later we put it in the field of the apparatus again. It went into a deep sleep — far deeper than normal hibernation. I was not able to reawaken it.

Q. Anything else?

A. Yes. There's an odd sort of half memory. I feel almost sure, that at some time I injected that cat — it was the only one with those markings — with anti-hibernine.

Q. But you have already told us that you tried to reawaken it.

A. Yes. But this memory is different.

Q. Anti-hibernine — that is the drug used on human beings, is it not?

A. Yes. Hibernine is administered to patients undergoing deep narcotherapy. Anti-hibernine is used to awaken them.

Q. And both drugs are effective with mountain cats?

A. Yes. It has always been considered quite fantastic that alien life forms, the indigenous fauna of Carinthia, should have developed so closely parallel to the life forms of the Home Planet in all ways.

Q. Can you describe the apparatus used by Mr Fergus? You talk, for example, of its "field". What sort of field?

A. I am neither a physicist nor a spaceman.

Q. But you saw the apparatus.

A. Yes. And I travelled once by interstellar liner on a holiday cruise to Caribbea. Like the other passengers, I was shown around the ship — the control room, the engine rooms, and all the rest of it. The apparatus that Fergus built is like a scale model of a Mannschenn Drive Unit, but somehow with Carlottit Beacon antennae included. When it was running and you were anywhere near it there was that queer I-have-been-here-before feeling. Fergus talked about the temporal field and temporal precession.

Q. And you think that by use of this "temporal precession" Mr Fergus was able to convince a hibernating mountain cat that it was last spring or next spring, or able to convince an awake and lively one that it was winter?

A. No. I don't think that that was what he was driving at.

Q. Why not.

A. Hibernine is absolutely safe, sure and dirt-cheap. Even when used in conjunction with deep freeze for a long sleep it's still cheap. In a hundred years a long-sleep unit would consume far less power than Fergus' machine gobbles in five minutes.

Q. Have you any idea of the real nature of his experiments?

A. No. But there seemed to be some sort of . . . of compulsion? I felt that with him there was some great personal urgency. I did think at first that it was the secret of immortality that he was after. But what's the use of immortality if you're going to spend it in hibernation?

Q. Would you say that Mr Fergus is fanatical?

A. Yes.

Q. As a scientist?

A. No. In a religious way.

Q. Religious?

A. Yes. Now and again, before we fell out, he'd have me drinking with him. He always kept a stock of imported Scotch — the real stuff, not that paint remover from Nova Caledon. After he'd had a few drinks he'd start comparing himself with Dr Faustus. I thought at first that this Faustus was a scientist, then that he was some sort of religious leader. Then, one day, I had to take the dustsled into Pilsen for stores, and I spent an hour or so in the library.

Q. Go on.

A. It seems that this Dr Faustus was an alchemist, back on the Home Planet, thousands of years ago. He was old, and he wanted his youth back, and he made some sort of a bargain with the Devil. The Devil came to collect his dues and Faustus tried to change sides at the last moment, and cried, "O Lord, put back Thy Universe, and give me back my yesterday . . ." and when I read that, I remembered that Fergus, when he was drunk, would always say that, or something like it. "Bring back yesterday."

Q. I cannot see how the legendary Dr Faustus has become involved in modern scientific research.

A. I'm just telling things the way they happened. As I say, this Fergus is mad. He's just a cranky old spaceman who's made enough money to play around with crazy experiments.

Q. Crazy experiments? But you have been telling us that something happened as a result of these same experiments.

A. That doesn't make them any less crazy. The craziness of it all got too much for me, and I had to leave.

Q. I suggest that the real reason for your leaving was a quarrel with Mr Fergus.

A. I suppose it could have been.

Q. His daughter, Elspeth, is very attractive, I believe.

A. If you happen to like that type. I prefer my women less snooty, with more meat on them.

Q. Your personal preferences didn't stop you from —

A. That's a lie! Anyhow, she encouraged me.

Technician: Look at the graph, Jan! Practically a straight line until your last two questions! After all that he's entitled to a few lies about the personal side of it.

A. I'm not lying.

Q. The machine does not lie, Mr Kravenko. Anyhow, thank you for your co-operation. [*Aside*] Run this through the analyser as soon as you can, Oscar.

Chapter Ten

STEVE RAISED his heavy eyebrows, looked at me. "Well?" he asked.

"Odd," I admitted.

"It's enough to get Central Intelligence all hot and bothered," he said flatly.

"So?"

"So it's up to Stefan Vynalek, Incorporated to find out just what is cooking on the Moon. It's up to the most recently recruited operative of the firm to do the finding out."

"I suppose it is," I admitted, with a sudden lack of reluctance. "But how do I set about it? You're the old hand, Steve. I'm just the new boy, the makee-learnee gumshoe."

He grinned. "At least you've picked up the jargon. Now, first of all, we have to get you on the Moon. That's simple. My secretary will proceed to the booking office of Moon Ferries tomorrow morning and will purchase a ticket for tomorrow night's rocket."

"A return ticket, I hope."

He ignored this. "The real problem is what you will be doing on the Moon. Even if a Distressed Terran Spaceman had money to throw away, he wouldn't throw it away on a busman's holiday. However, I have considered that angle. You will go to the Moon as an operative of this firm, on the firm's business. Ostensibly, you are employed by Mrs Kravik, who has reason to suspect that her husband, who is spending a few weeks in Pilsen drawing up plans for the new spaceport, is straying from the straight and narrow path. The Kraviks, as it happens, are good friends of mine and have no objection to their name being used in this way."

"But why the smokescreen?" I asked. "As far as I've gathered, Fergus is a virtual hermit."

"His daughter is not. Besides, I have reason to suspect that powerful private interests are also intrigued by Fergus' research."

"So I go to the Moon," I said. "I make a show of investigating this Kravik character. Meanwhile, I get into Fergus' chamber of horrors somehow and find out what he's playing at. Should I fall foul of the civil authorities I go to jail, I suppose."

"You do. But I'll have you sprung before you get too tired of beans and water."

"Thanks."

"Don't mention it."

"One point — you said something about the powerful private interests who might be involved. What if they want to play rough? Do I get to pack a rod?"

"A rod?"

"Pocket artillery, if you like. I got the word from one of your damned books."

He said thoughtfully, "It might be well. I suppose you can handle small arms?"

"I can. All space officers hold commissions in the Reserve and the use of lethal ironmongery comes into the training."

"All right. I can supply a rod, with shoulder holster. And I'll see to it that you get a spot of practice in the police shooting gallery tomorrow. Anything else?"

"Plenty. I suppose you have photographs of this Fergus character and his daughter."

"Of course." He got up, went through into the laboratory, came back with a carton. "Here you are. All recent. All taken by means of the Central Intelligence spy beam."

I spilled the little plastic cubes out on to the polished surface of the low table. I picked the first one up. In it was the tiny spacesuited figure of a man. Luckily the suit had a goldfish-bowl helmet, so it was possible to distinguish his features.

"That's the only one of Fergus," Steve told me. "He

rarely comes out of the dome, and the interior, as you know, is blanked out by the blocker."

"So this is Fergus," I said. I looked at the face of the little image — the lean, haggard face under the untidy mop of white hair. It had to be Fergus — or it had to be any senior interstellar drive engineer. Any spaceman seeing it could have told at once what this man Fergus was, or had been. The Mannschenn Drive gives all its servants that far-seeing look — far-seeing in time, not in space.

"The others are of his daughter," said Steve.

I looked at them with rather more enthusiasm. There was, first of all, a shot of her, spacesuited, boarding a weird, boatlike contraption that I took to be one of the dustsleds. Then there were the other shots of her, in street clothes, that must have been taken during a visit by her to Pilsen, the city not far from the Fergus dome. No photograph, two- or three-dimensional, can do full justice to a beautiful woman. But one or two of the solidographs, taken, as they had been, by an Intelligence technician and not by an artist, did capture, slightly and fortuitously, the elusive, four-dimensional quality that is the true essence of beauty. But there was something familiar about her. That red-gold hair was wrong, but the long, slender legs under the brief shorts were right, and so were the breasts, definite but not obtrusive, revealed by the thin jersey. And the face — thin, finely featured — was almost right.

"Ilona," I whispered.

"What was that?" demanded Steve sharply.

"A very attractive girl," I said.

"Yes. Isn't she. Not too meaty — as Mr. Kravenko has already told us."

"Damn Kravenko."

"Jealous? You aren't thinking of mixing pleasure with business, are you?"

"No," I lied.

"Hm. Well, you'd better come through to the lab. I'll see what I can find for you in the way of a gun."

Reluctantly, I put the solidographs back into the carton, followed him into the laboratory. He had the door of a big metal cabinet open. I looked inside it to the racked weapons. "Quite an arsenal," I said.

He took down one of the pistols. "Perhaps the Minetti five millimetre would be the best for you."

"No. Make it the Webley ten millimetre."

"The Minetti magazine holds twenty round, and I doubt if you'll be fighting any long-range actions."

"The Webley has a firing stud and not a trigger, and a spacesuited man can fire it. Furthermore, you can slip in a fresh magazine quite easily even when you're wearing space gauntlets."

"Any more reasons?" he asked rather acidly.

"Yes. It's the handgun we're taught to use during our Reserve training."

"You win."

He handed me the gun, and while I was getting the heft of it he opened a drawer and pulled out a shoulder holster. He told me to take off my jacket, strapped the thing in place over my shirt. The gun slid into it easily. I flattered myself that with a little practice I could make it slip out just as easily — but whether or not I'd have it pointing in the right direction after I'd slipped it out was another matter.

"And a side holster," I said.

"Damn it all, Johnnie, do you think I'm fitting you out to fight a private war?"

"Yes."

"But what do you want a side holster for?"

"You told me that I might have to work in a spacesuit; that's why you wanted me for the job. A shoulder holster would not be practicable wear under a spacesuit, and would be hardly better over one. So. . . ."

"Oh, all right, all right." He found a side holster for the Webley. "And now for the really big important items of your armament."

"I already have a watch," I started to say, then saw that

the two little objects were not wristwatches.

"Minicamera," he said. "Minirecorder. There's no need for you to flash them around unnecessarily. On the other hand, there's no need for you to make a dreadful secret of them. Lots of people carry them, especially tourists. And they'll be quite in character with what you're supposed to be. They are just what the well-dressed private eye wears, especially when he's after divorce evidence."

"Hmm. Ingenious."

"And simple. And sensitive. The recorder will hear a pin drop at twenty meters. The camera will take clear pictures in almost pitch darkness, or even in pitch darkness as long as there's a little infrared radiation. When you get inside the Fergus dome, record everything."

"If Fergus lets me."

"That's up to you."

I accompanied him back to the sitting room and fresh drinks, feeling a little like a perambulating Christmas tree.

He said, "There's still time for you to back out, John."

I lifted one of the little solidographs of Elspeth Fergus out of the box, held it in the palm of my hand.

I said, "I'll stick."

He said, "Yes, that's always a good way to forget a woman, isn't it?"

"Is it?" I looked at the graceful figurine. *You're lovely, but you aren't Ilona.*

"But remember, you're on a job of work. For me. And for the Government."

"I'm grateful for the job," I told him.

Suddenly he looked worried.

"I hope you stay that way, John. I hope you stay that way."

Chapter Eleven

"ILONA," I began.

The little screen went dead, but she had switched off only the visual transmission from her end.

"Yes?" she snapped.

"It's John."

"I'm not blind. What do you want?"

"I'm leaving tonight."

There was a flicker of interest in her voice. "Where for?"

"The Moon. Wenceslaus, that is."

"Oh. Is that all? The way you're carrying on I thought it must be the Lesser Magellanic Cloud at least."

"I thought —"

"Goodbye," she said, with an air of definite finality.

I stood before the instrument for what seemed a long time, realizing at least the futility of punching her number again. I left the office then, rejoining Steve Vynalek and Liz Bartok in the shabbily furnished lounge of the Hostel, tried to convey the impression of jaunty unconcern.

"Get through?" asked Liz.

"Yes," I said.

"A pity," she said.

"What do you mean?" I demanded.

"You know, Johnnie."

Steve looked at his watch, remarked, "Time you were getting aboard, John."

"I suppose so," I said.

Liz filled three small glasses. "What is that archaic Terran expression?" she asked. "A stirrup cup?"

"All the best, John," said Steve.

"All the best, Johnnie," said Liz.

"Thanks," I said.

Suddenly I realized that I didn't want to leave Carinthia, that I was trying to spin out my last few minutes on the planet. There was, I suppose the wild hope that Ilona would relent, that she would call me back at the Hostel. There was the even wilder hope that she would hurry out to Port Tauber.

"You have to go," said Liz.

"Not far," I said. "Not for long."

She looked at me sadly, shook her head, started to say something.

"What was that?" asked Steve sharply.

"Nothing," she said.

"All right. Let's go."

I picked up my briefcase and overnight bag — the heavier baggage was already aboard the ship — and walked with my two friends out of the Hostel, over the scarred concrete towards *Moonmaiden*. She looked pitifully small and fragile standing there in the glare of the floodlights, dwarfed by the gantries and belts that were now withdrawing from her, the last few tons of cargo and stores having been onloaded. The red light atop her needle stem was winking — the red light that illogically (although there is historical logic) carries the name of Blue Peter. On the spaceport control tower a similar red light was flashing.

We paused at the foot of the ramp, looked up to the after airlock. A uniformed spaceman stood in the little compartment. He saw Liz, waved to her and then came down the ramp to the apron.

"Ivor," said Liz, "this is Johnnie Petersen. He's travelling with you. Johnnie, this is Ivor Radek, second officer."

We shook hands.

"Pity you couldn't have got a passage in the *Queen* or the *Princess*," said Radek. "They're rather more like the sort of ship that you're accustomed to."

"Don't believe him, Johnnie," said Liz. "They're just like the *Maiden* here, no more than Moon ferries."

"But they *are* passenger ships," Radek insisted. He winked. "There are a few glamorous blondes aboard, usually.".

"Ivor," explained Liz, "was third officer of *Moon Queen* before he was promoted."

"Promoted? It might be promotion if this little brute carried a third. But she doesn't."

"How many passengers?" I asked.

"We have accommodation for twelve, but you're the only one this trip."

"Mr Radek!" shouted a voice from the airlock.

"Sir?"

"Get this airlock secured as soon as you can!"

"Aye, aye, sir!"

"If you get in a real jam, Johnnie," said Steve, "don't forget to yell for help."

"I'll not forget."

"Goodbye, Johnnie," said Liz. She embraced me briefly and, once again, I wondered how I had ever thought that there was anything motherly about her.

"Mr Radek!" bawled the voice from the airlock again.

"All right, break it up, you people," said the second mate briskly. "We have to get this tin can upstairs some time tonight."

I preceded Radek up the ramp. The officer standing at the head of it, the mate, nodded to me, then beckoned to a uniformed girl and ordered, "Miss Bentz, please show this gentleman to his cabin."

"This way, sir," she said pleasantly.

I followed her into the axial shaft, up the spiral stairway. In such a small ship an elevator would have been a fantastic luxury. Spacemanlike, I noted the various flats and levels as we climbed inside the ship. There were the cargo holds. There was a gyroscope flat, but there was not, of course, an interstellar drive flat on the next level. Neither was there a hydroponics flat, a "farm". This struck me as being strange, then I realized that a Moon ferry would have no need for such equipment, that for a short run sufficient food and water would be carried in the ship's stores, that internal atmosphere would be purified by chemical means and refreshed from oxygen cylinders.

We came to the passenger flat with its six double-berth cabins arranged around the central well, the half-dozen wedge shaped cells. I peered dubiously through the door that the stewardess slid open.

"Have you travelled before, sir?" she asked politely.

"Yes," I told her, but I was pleased that she had asked the question. Presumably only Radek, who was a friend of Liz, knew that I was a spaceman. And I was a spaceman in bad odour, so the fewer people aboard this ship who knew my background the better. "Yes," I said. "But only in interstellar ships."

She flashed me a brief smile. "Then you may find this just a little strange. Your hand baggage goes into this locker for blast-off. You lie on the bunk, of course. . . ."

I realized that she was waiting for me to stretch out on the bunk.

"And then this webbing goes over you."

I submitted to her deft ministrations.

"Secure safety webbing," blurted a P.A. speaker suddenly. "Secure safety webbing. Count down for blast-off commencing."

"Damn!" swore the girl. "The Old Man — the captain — is always in a hurry. I'll have to ride up with you. Do you mind?"

"Not a bit," I said, and then was rather disappointed when, instead of sharing my bunk, she stretched out on the other one, pulling the webbing over her body with practised ease, snapping the buckle shut.

"Ten," said the voice from the speaker. "Nine . . . eight. . . ."

"Have to do the first fifty kilometers on chemical fuel," said the girl. "That's why we have heavy acceleration."

"Four . . . three . . . two . . . one. . . . Fire!"

There was nothing to it. Even medium acceleration in a control-room chair can be exhausting, possibly painful. This way, it was riding to the sky in luxury. Being a passenger, I decided, had much to recommend it.

61

Chapter Twelve

IT WAS a short voyage, and, at first, a boring one.

Moonmaiden, by big ship standards, was pitifully undermanned — captain, two mates (who also handled communications), two engineers and the overworked but cheerful Miss Bentz who, as well as being stewardess, was also the purser. Nobody had any time to spare for social intercourse; watch-and-watch routine means that the officers concerned spend their watches below in catching up on their sleep.

This state of affairs was, in some ways, advantageous. I had ample time to myself and was able to spend it reading. I read and reread all the documents that Steve had given me concerning Fergus; his history, until he began to make the series of investments that made his fortune, could have been the history of any senior interstellar drive engineer. Technical education at M.I.T. on Earth, specializing in Mannschenn Drive mechanics. Service with Trans-Galactic Clippers as probationary junior engineer, fifth interstellar drive engineer, fourth, third, second, chief. A refresher course at M.I.T. — Carlotti Beacon and Communications Systems, Principles and Maintenance. Marriage to Carlotta MacInnes, citizen of Nova Caledon, whom he first met when she was travelling to Earth as a passenger in *James Baines*. (So, I thought rather bitterly, some shipboard romances turn out well.)

Continued service in *James Baines*. And then, quite suddenly, resignation from the employ of Trans-Galactic Clippers. Period of apparent unemployment, and period of gambling. Kentucky Derby, Melbourne Cup, Solar System Welterweight Championship and other sporting events — and all of them sporting events in which men or animals won against long odds. Period of stock exchange gambling — the purchase of shares in small companies, that, owing to new discoveries, made fortunes, and not small ones, either, for themselves and their shareholders. Nickname on the stock exchange: Farseeing Fergus.

Birth of daughter, Elspeth Fergus. Continued prosperity. Purchase of laboratory on Moon — Earth's moon, that is. Purchase from Interstellar Transport Commission of Mannshenn Drive and Carlotti Beacon equipment. Luxury apartment in Luna City, but Fergus spending practically all his time in laboratory. Hasty trip from Luna City by Fergus, discovery of only daughter in apartment. Fergus, according to witness — baby sitter — almost frantic, telephoning friends and places of entertainment trying, unsuccessfully, to locate Mrs Fergus. Acutely conscious of and perturbed by passage of time. Finally, in state of near desperation, leaving apartment with daughter, taking her in tractor back to laboratory, making exit from city airlock seconds prior to crash of Lunar Ferry *Selene* on main dome of Luna City. Many fatal casualties, including Mrs Fergus. Allegations made that Fergus had foreseen future, had warned nobody, had tried to save only own family. Cryptic remark made to reporter: "I remembered, but too late." Press campaign against Fergus, demands for governmental investigation of laboratory. Destruction of laboratory by explosion. Demands that Fergus be held for interrogation. Hasty departure of Fergus and daughter from Earth.

Short period on Lao, minor satellite of Si Kiang, capital planet of Flammarion's Cluster, establishment of new laboratory on Lao. Rise of Maleter Dictatorship. (Anybody with that name, I thought, would be a natural dictator. Wonder if he's any relation. . . .) Interest by Maleter's secret police in Fergus' researches. Escape by Fergus and daughter in small private spacecraft from Lao. Failure of time-fused bomb to explode, and seizure of laboratory by secret police. Revolution, seizure of Lao by insurgent naval forces. Destruction of Lao by nuclear missiles from Si Kiang.

Brief periods on Waverley, Elsinore and Thule. Sequence of events remarkably similar: hasty departures prior to freak accidents destroying laboratories. Long period on Caribbea, research apparently abandoned, all efforts devoted, with spectacular success, to rebuilding of personal fortune.

Fergus once again rich. Departure for Carinthia, purchase of site and building of laboratory on Wenceslaus. Purchase of Mannschenn Drive and Carlotti Beacon components from Interstellar Transport Commission's stores at Port Tauber. Purchase of controlling interest in New Prague Furriers, arrangements made for live trapping of mountain cats and their transport to Wenceslaus. Employment of Kravenko to care for livestock. Dismissal of Kravenko. Interrogation of Kravenko by Central Intelligence.

It all added up to . . . something.

But what?

It all added up, I decided, to prevision. There was the gambling, by means of which Fergus had made at least two considerable fortunes. There was the valuable ability to be elsewhere whenever disaster struck — the *Selene* catastrophe, the Cluster Revolt, the Waverley Comet. I tried to envisage some fantastic rig incorporating a crystal ball, a Mannschenn Drive unit and Carlotti Beacon antennae. Fantastic rig, I decided, was just the right phrase.

But Central Intelligence had the idea that Fergus could travel back in time — back, not forward — and that his invention could be used to change history. Central Intelligence, I decided, was barking up the wrong tree.

But it was not for me to theorize. I was just a spaceman, pure and simple. Simple, anyhow. All that I had to do was to effect an entry into the Fergus dome, to see and to observe, and to report what I saw and observed to those who could turn the data into a nice, complicated equation and then come up with a nice, uncomplicated answer.

I had learned all that I could about Fergus. It was a pity that there was so little material on his daughter. What were her tastes in food and drink and entertainment?

Steve had slipped up badly there. He hadn't lived up to the principles expounded in those archaic books that he maintained should be the Bible of the modern private eye. *"Cherchez la femme,"* they said, almost all of them. *"Cherchez la femme.* And when you've found her, use her."

All that remained, then, was a study of the terrain over which I should be operating. I found Miss Bentz in her office, filling in those forms that are considered essential by port officials the galaxy over. She looked up from her paper work with a certain relief.

"Miss Bentz," I said, "have you a library aboard this hooker?"

"We have," she said. She smiled sympathetically. "There's nothing much to do here but read, is there?"

"There's not," I agreed.

"I'm afraid that our stock of books isn't a very good one. If you like I'll see what the officers have."

"Don't bother. The book I want is almost bound to be in the ship's library. Just a guidebook to Wenceslaus."

"We have one," she said, "but it's fearfully out of date. There's no mention of the Sudeten Dome, or of the new spaceport that's in the course of construction at Pilsen."

"I think it will do," I said, "for what I want. This will be my first time on your moon, and I just want to get some sort of general idea as to what conditions are like."

"Just wait here," she told me.

She was back in a couple of minutes, holding a slim volume. "This," she told me, "is it."

"Thanks."

She said. "But a book's not much good. You really want somebody who *knows* Wenceslaus to tell you about it."

I asked, "Do you know Wenceslaus?"

"Do I not!" she replied. "Join the Carinthian Space Service and see the wonders of alien planets! I started on the Silesian run — and Silesia is nothing but a dirty great slag heap. As soon as I had enough seniority I belly-ached for a berth in a Moon ferry. At least here, I get plenty of time in New Prague. Trouble is, I joined the Space Service too late. It was all right when Carinthia was still a full member of the Federation; in those days Carinthian nationals — like Liz Bartok — could ship out in the starwagons, Trans-Galactic Clippers and the I.T.C. ships. But now every vessel of Federation registry must carry Federation personnel only."

"There's always the Rim," I told her.

"Nor for me," she said definitely.

"Thanks for the book," I said.

"Think nothing of it. And, as I said, somebody who knows Wenceslaus could tell you much more."

I looked at her appraisingly and remembered my thoughts on the subject of *cherchez la femme*. She wasn't bad at all. But then, she was Carinthian. On most planets she'd have been considered something special. I don't know what it is about Carinthian climate or environment or whatever produces that Siamese-cat quality in the women, but I've always liked cats in general and Siamese cats in particular.

"I shall have got through all this bumf after dinner," she said, gesturing towards the papers on her desk.

I got in some reading:
Wenceslaus.
Only satellite of Carinthia.
Atmosphere: Hard vacuum.
Density: 1.5
Gravity: 0.15
Flora: None.
Fauna: Likewise.
And so on.
And so forth.

"You're from Earth," she said.

"How did you know?" I asked stupidly.

"I've been all day filling in forms, silly. Forms about the

ship. Forms about the cargo. Forms about our one and only passenger — you."

"Oh."

"And in any case, Ivor's told me about you."

"Oh?"

"And, in any case, second mates of luxury liners don't miss their ships every day of the week, Johnnie. You have a certain notoriety."

"I suppose that's why the Old Man and the mate treat me like something the cat brought in."

"You suppose right."

"Aren't you liable to get into trouble, Anna?"

"No. I take my —" She grinned. "Sorry. What I should have said was that I know rather too much about the rackets that my so-called superiors are involved in. If *I* go, *they* go."

I looked at her as she reclined on the other berth of my little cabin, thinking that women aboard ships, crew or passengers, were far too dangerous. Especially women like Ilona. And like Anna. There was something of Ilona about her . . . .

I transferred my attention to the low table that she had set between us; the table with the bottle of the inevitable Slivovitz, the plate of canapes. I started to count my blessings, and one of them was being able to enjoy a drink with an attractive girl whilst in space, without having to adopt the infantile expedient of sucking from bottles. There was something to be said for service in the despised puddle-jumpers. *Moonmaid*, for example, would maintain steady acceleration until turnover, and then would maintain steady deceleration until touchdown. There was propellant to spare, and no interstellar drive in operation to make any change of the ship's mass impossible.

I looked at her again, and liked what I saw. She had contrived to make her uniform very un-uniform. The top button of her shirt was undone. Her shorts may once have been tailored in accordance with the regulations, but they had been shortened since that initial tailoring. Some women should be forbidden by law to wear shorts. She was not one of them.

I remembered Ilona, and the circumstances of our parting. I remembered Liz, and what she had offered that I was unable to take. I remembered Ilona, and thought that Anna could almost have been her sister. I forgot Ilona, and shifted into a more comfortable position.

"You Earthlings are lucky," she said.

"Why, Anna?"

"You've got a moon that *is* a moon. I've seen pictures of it. There's scenery. All those mountains. All those craters. And even from Earth you can see some of the features. I tell you Johnnie, that there's no romance in being out in the moonlight when the moon is no more than a big, blank, shining ball in the sky."

"Then what's Wenceslaus like?" I asked dutifully, rather reluctant to shunt her train of thought on to unromantic tracks.

"Just a big ball of dust. Fine dust, almost fluid. You could sink right down in it if you weren't wearing dust-shoes. And you'd drown if you weren't wearing a spacesuit."

"And you'd asphyxiate without one," I pointed out.

"Shut up. And if your suit radio went on the blink you'd suffocate, anyhow, when your air ran out, with nobody knowing where you were or where to start digging for you."

"Our moon is dusty in parts," I said.

"In parts, perhaps. But Wenceslaus is dusty all over. The buildings aren't buildings; they're rafts. They're just floating on the surface. And the dustsleds are really boats."

"And how do they work?" I asked. "The book didn't go into details."

"Like a jet plane. They suck in the dust at one end and blow it out at the other. Electrostatic charge. Almost like the ion drive used by some spaceships."

"Ingenious."

She said suddenly, "Your glass is empty, Johnnie."

She got to her feet like a great, sinuous cat, and with the motion the second button of her shirt came undone. She stepped gracefully over the low table, sank down beside me. Her face was very close to mine, her lips inviting.

I hesitated. And then, suddenly, I was sure.

The buttons of her shirt were all undone now, and the garment was falling from her slim shoulders, her pointed, pink-nippled breasts. As I buried my face between them her hands were busy with the fastenings of my clothing, and my own free hand had found the press-seam of her shorts. I was lost in the urgency of it all, and so was she, and neither of us noticed when the bunk lurched beneath us, the lights flickered.

Then, with a crash, the table overturned as the lights went out, and with the sudden darkness came the strident clangour of alarm bells.

Chapter Thirteen

THERE ARE two golden rules for survival in space: If you know what is wrong, then do something about it; if you don't know what is wrong, then don't do anything until you *do* know what is wrong.

Obviously, on this occasion, the first rule did not apply. I was well aware of that, and so was Anna. For what seemed a long time we sat there in the darkness, still holding each other, still close, but as two human beings needing warmth and comfort in the hostile night rather than as lovers. And then, suddenly, we were no longer sitting. All sensation of weight was gone. We were floating. Abruptly the clamour of the alarm ceased and we realized that the muffled thunder of the reaction drive, the subdued roar that had become the background to our lives, was silent.

I said, "We can still breathe."

"There seems to be no appreciable reduction of air pressure," agreed Anna.

"The drive," I said, "was shut down well after the explosion, or whatever it was, so the damage probably isn't in the engine room. Was it a meteorite, do you think?"

"No. The Carinthian system is singularly free from such cosmic debris."

I laughed at the absurd pedantry of her words. She made a noise like an angry cat and pushed away from me. I heard her making a peculiar choking sound (was she crying? I wondered) and heard the rustling of her garments as she dressed.

"Damn you," she muttered sullenly, "where are my shorts?"

"Never mind your shorts," I told her. "Let's try to get things sorted out. First, whatever happened didn't happen in the engine room. Secondly, whatever happened didn't hole the hull, or, if it did, the airtight doors functioned efficiently."

She made that odd choking sound in reply.

"You're a spacewoman," I said sharply. "You're an officer of this ship. Snap out of it!"

"I'm perfectly all right," she said coldly, and not very convincingly.

"Then tell me this. Does this ship have an emergency lighting system?"

"Of course."

"Then why isn't it working?"

"I'm not an engineer," she mumbled.

I groped my way past her, felt a surge of anger as naked flesh shrank away from my touch. I found the door to the locker at the head of my bunk, got it open, fumbled for my briefcase. I pulled out what I was looking for, my pencil torch. I switched it on, adjusting to broad beam.

Anna cursed me, but made no effort to hide her partial nudity.

I looked at her. Her face was pale, beaded with perspiration. Her hands came up to cover her mouth as she choked and gulped. For a long moment I found this spectacle of an obviously spacesick spacewoman hard to accept, then realized that these short-hop rocketeers, these puddle-jumpers, would be affected by free fall as badly as any planetlubber. But, I thought, they must have some experience of free fall. The ship falls free during turnover.

"In — in the locker . . ." she gasped. "A bottle. Held by clips. Pills. . . ."

I had seen the bottle, had assumed that it, with its contents, had been put there merely for the comfort and convenience of queasy passengers. I unscrewed the cap, shook out two of the little pellets. Anna snatched them from my hand, brought her own hand rapidly to her mouth. She lost the pills before she had even started to swallow them. I gave her two more.

This time she managed to get and keep them down. Slowly her face regained its colour. She said, "I'm sorry."

I grunted.

She said, "On this run, with constant acceleration, we never experience free fall. Or hardly ever. We take these just before turnover, or if we know that the drive is going to be shut down for any other reason."

"I'll believe you. Get dressed, then we'll see what's wrong."

She was dressed before I was. While she was waiting for me she did her best to clear up the mess with a soft towel. I was glad that she did. My own space butterfly hunting days began and ended while I was still a first-trip cadet.

"And now what?" she asked as I ran my finger up the press-seam of my slacks.

"You'd better stay here," I told her.

"This is my ship!" she flared.

"All right. Come along. I'm going forward."

She would be a nuisance, I thought, untrained as she was in handling herself in free fall. She would be a nuisance, but I couldn't leave her there, alone in a dark cabin in a crippled ship. And, in any case, she knew the vessel better than I did.

Pushing off from the outboard wall of the cabin, the ship's side, I floated to the sliding door. Gripping one of the bunk stanchions with my right hand, I had the purchase to pull the door open with my left. There were handrails in the alleyway outside — the alleyway that was a gallery around the axial shaft — so I was able to make my way to the nearest door giving ingress to the shaft with relative ease, delayed only by having to wait for Anna, who was carrying the torch.

I took the light from her before we entered the shaft, stuck it into my belt. I ignored the spiral staircase; if there is any more awkward obstacle to negotiate in free fall it has yet to be discovered. I jumped to the central column — it was no more than a slender bar — pulled myself forward. I could hear the sound of Anna's breathing behind me, knew that she wasn't doing too badly.

We passed the public rooms flat and the officers' flat, came to the end of the column. Forward of it the way was blocked by an airtight door. Beyond that door was Control. The pressure gauge, the face of which was flush with the metal surface, registered an uncompromising zero.

"Who would have been in control at this time?" I demanded.

"Igor," replied Anna hesitantly. "It was his watch. Perhaps the captain."

"Control's had it," I said. "But there are the others — the engineer and the officer off duty."

"They should be out," she whispered.

"I know damned well they should be out and about. Those bloody alarm bells of yours must have been heard on the Rim! There must be something wrong with them."

There was.

We retraced our way to the officers' flat and found that both doors opening to the axial shaft were tightly sealed, tightly locked. We found another air-pressure gauge, and if it was to be believed — and, desperately as we wished to disbelieve we could not ignore that needle, hard against the stop, that ominous black numeral — there was hard vacuum inside the officers' accommodation.

"Who's in the engine room?" I demanded.

"The second."

"Then what the hell is he playing at? Come on!"

I jumped out to the central column again, pulled myself rapidly aft, through the various levels. At the end of the column the airtight door to the machinery was shut, and I groaned. I shone my torch on the face of the gauge, and felt more cheerful. There was normal pressure behind the door. I tapped the thick glass with my finger and the needle didn't budge.

"There are manual controls," said Anna.

"Good. Show me."

She showed me.

The controls were not of a type with which I was familiar, and the handwheel-operated worm gear was maddeningly slow in operation. But at last the door was open and I was shining the torch into the dark compartment, onto the gleaming metal of machines, the glittering glass of gauges, the glistening globules of fluid that swirled slowly around the faintly stirring shape in the white overalls.

"Another one!" I ejaculated angrily. "Can't any of you people take free fall without spewing your guts up?"

"Nikki!" called Anna sharply. "Nikki!"

A groan answered her.

I groaned too, as I pulled myself into that noiseome engine room. I pulled the engineer clear of his mess, shook him. He started to struggle. I slapped his face, hard.

"Don't. Don't do that!" he gasped.

"I'll do it some more if you don't snap out of it. What about the lights?"

He gestured feebly. "Switchboard. . . ."

I let go of him, caught a stanchion, swung myself to the board. There was a button labelled: EMERGENCY LIGHTING. I pressed it. The lights came on. Ignoring the engineer and Anna, I looked around me. I found the intercom telephone. I called Control. There was no answer — but I wasn't expecting one. I called the captain, the chief officer, the chief engineer. I put the handset back in its clip.

As I turned away from the useless instrument I saw Anna taking something from the first-aid box, give it to the engineer. There was no need for me to ask what it was. I waited, not very patiently, for the pills to take effect. I struck a cigarette on my thumbnail, put the little cylinder to my mouth. Smoking, I knew, might well be a criminal waste of oxygen — we had yet to learn the full extent and nature of the damage to the ship — but I considered that it was justifiable in the circumstances.

"Why is the drive shut down?" I asked.

"I — I didn't know what had happened. I thought it might be safer." He said eagerly, "I'll restart it."

"You will not. Not until I find out where we are, how we're heading. Not until we find out what's wrong." I inhaled and exhaled tobacco smoke. "And why were the lights turned off?"

"I don't know. A fuse, perhaps. And then the jennies stopped."

"Why did the jennies stop?"

"They run off the waste heat from the drive."

"What a bloody ship!" I swore. "And why was your airtight door shut?"

"Listen, Mister!" he blustered. "You can't cross examine me. You're only a passenger."

"I happen," I told him, "to hold an Interstellar Master Astronaut's Certificate, and that, by galactic space law, puts me in charge of this vesel in the event of the death or incapacitation of her officers, regardless of my status or lack of it."

"Death?" he mumbled. "The Old Man? The chief? The mate?"

"What the hell do you think has been happening while you've been wallowing in your vomit? Something has happened to the entire fore end of this wagon, the control room, the officer's flat. And the first thing I want to do is find out what's happened. I suppose you keep a couple of suits in this bicycle shop?"

"In this locker," said Anna. She pulled one out. "Here."

I inspected it, swore. "Look at the bloody air gauge! Get the other one out and see if it's any better. I'm not going forward with only five minutes' breathing time!"

She flared, "There are men there who may be dying!"

"There are men there who are dead," I stated brutally. "*Dead*. Have you ever seen what hard vacuum does to a man? *I* have. I'm sorry, but we can't do anything to help them, and we'll not help ourselves by rushing in madly without adequate preparation. All we can hope to do is to save ourselves and to save the ship."

"Here's the other suit," said Anna.

"That's a little better," I told her. "And now, you, Nick, or whatever your name is, have you a plan of the layout of this vessel? One showing airtight doors and bulkheads?"

"What do you intend to do?" asked Anna.

"That's what I'm trying to find out," I said.

Chapter Fourteen

ONCE I had studied the plans it was possible to work out a plan of campaign. One snag, I discovered, was that *Moonmaiden* possessed no internal airlocks. Or, to be more exact, she possessed one, and one only, and that one a big one. It was the axial shaft.

"This is what I shall do," I told the engineer. "I shall put on this suit and make my way forward. You will shut your airtight door and then, when I give you the word, you will open the right valve and evacuate the air from the shaft."

"It's a lot of atmosphere to lose," he said dubiously.

"There are only three of us to breathe what will be left," I pointed out. "And, in any case, the automatic doors to the unholed compartments will shut as soon as the pressure in the shaft starts falling."

"And how will you give the word?" asked Anna.

"You wear the other suit," I told her, "but leave the visor open. I'll keep in touch with you by suit radio."

"And what if the radio fails after you get outside? How shall I know when to pressurize the shaft again when you want to come back?"

"We'll make a real spacewoman of you yet," I said approvingly. "Always look on the gloomy side of things, and then work out ways to cope with it. Well, if the radio fails, and if I want to come back into the engine room, I'll rap sharply three times on the door."

I climbed into the suit with the full tanks, snapped the helmet visor shut. This was the first time that I had worn a spacesuit since the last emergency drill in *Lightning* — how long ago? Chronologically it wasn't such a long time, but a lot had happened since then. There had been Ilona. . . . And why, I wondered, do I have to start thinking about her now, of all times?

"Testing," I said. "one, two, three. . . . The Leith

police dismisseth us."

"I hear you," sad the tinny little voice in my helmet phones, "loud and clear."

"All right. Tell your boyfriend that I'm going out now."

Indignantly: "He's no boyfriend of mine!"

"Tell him anyhow."

"All right." There was a pause. "And be careful, Johnnie."

I walked to the ladder under the doorway, the magnetized soles of the suit giving the illusion of gravity. I climbed the ladder, and the illusion vanished. Climbing, with no weight to lift, is not climbing. I eased myself through the aperture, reached for and grasped the long, slender pillar of the central column, pulled myself clear of the hatch.

"Anna," I said, "close airtight door. Open valve."

"Close airtight door," she repeated. "Open valve."

Looking past my feet, I saw the engine room door slide shut. I transferred my attention to the external pressure gauge on the left wrist of my suit, saw the needle quiver and begin to fall. "Evacuation commenced," I reported. Then, after what seemed a long time, "Evacuation complete."

Hand over hand I went along the column. As I passed the various levels I looked from side to side, noted all doors were shut. Not too much atmosphere would have been lost. But, I asked myself, did it matter? Finally I came to the bulkhead between the forward end of the shaft and the control room. To open this door, however, took far longer than it had taken to open the one aft; bare hands are better working tools than hands in heavy gloves.

My first impression, as I pulled myself into the control room, was one of blinding light. Nearly directly ahead was a huge, featureless sphere, a vast hard, white radiance that almost completely blotted out the blackness of space. Nearly directly ahead. . . . That was all to the good. I should have time to work, time to bring things under some sort of control — if I could. And if I couldn't? Then we

77

should swing around the Moon and fall back to Carinthia, and, presumably, the Port Pilsen radar operators would realize that something was seriously amiss and a tug would be sent to take us in charge before the crash.

Nearly directly ahead . . . .

It's a long, long time since you were a first-trip cadet, Petersen, I told myself. It's a long, long time since you learned that a spaceship is aimed not at where a celestial body is, but at where it will be.

Anna's voice came as interruption to my thoughts. "Johnnie. . . ."

"In Control," I said curtly. "Investigating."

"Ivor," she whispered. "And the captain — are they . . .?"

"Yes," I said brutally. There was no need for hesitation. Every viewport was smashed, and the metal frames were grotesquely twisted.

But there were no bodies. There was no debris whatsoever. When the air had gone out of the control room in one explosive gasp it had taken everything with it that had not been secured. But, I thought, if a meteorite holed one port, the others should still be intact . . . . (I was still not believing Anna's claim that there were no meteorites in the Carinthian system.)

Meteorites or no meteorites, there had been something solid, something hard, moving in that control room at high velocity. The radar was inoperable; the screens had been smashed in, the console holed in half a dozen places. I went to the control panels set before the captain's and chief officer's chairs, found similar damage. And the controls were dead. Even with the ship in her present crippled state they should have been alive with lights — airtight door indicators, compartment pressure indicators. Reaction drive indicators . . . .

"Johnnie," came Anna's voice again. "Are you all right?"

"Yes."

Absently, I pulled a shard of grey metal from the

upholstery of the chairs. It was twisted, jagged; I had to exert force to work it loose. There was lettering on it: . . . CEIVER MARK IV.

*Trans*ceiver?

I walked to the radio, my feet sliding stickily over the deck. Actually, to where the radio had been. There was the pedestal, oddly flattened, and a few shreds of grey metal casing splayed outwards. There was the ragged gash in the deck beneath it, the gash through which the atmosphere of the officers' quarters must have escaped.

Transceivers don't explode.

But this one had.

"Johnnie!"

"All right, all right," I snapped. "The control room's a mess. No survivors."

"And the accommodation?"

"Holed. There'll be no survivors there."

"How can you be sure?"

"I am sure."

(Freak accidents are common enough in space; freak survivals are extremely rare.)

I looked out through the shattered ports, to that ghastly white sphere. It was larger. It had swollen appreciably even in the few minutes I had been in the control room. It was larger. It was too large. I tried to remember what the Old Man had grunted to me over the dinner table; grudgingly he had told me the time of turnover, the E.T.A. We must be well past the turnover point now; against that, however, we had ceased to accelerate very shortly after the accident. The accident? I looked again at what was left of the transceiver.

Something had to be done, and soon. That was obvious. But what? And how?

I recalled my last drill with the Reserve. It had been taken up with a survival course of sorts, the problem being to land a crippled warship, her control room wrecked by enemy fire, on the surface of a presumably friendly planet. It had been, essentially, a course on "seat of the pants" piloting. After my session in the pilot's chair of the simulator I had been quite convinced that I had completed the destruction begun by the hostile gunnery, and the examiner had said nothing to dispel this conviction. Even so, perhaps here there were *some* instruments . . . .

I pulled myself into the captain's chair, strapped myself in. I poked a gloved finger at the PERISCOPE EXTENSION button. The metallic fabric of the suit transmitted the faintest of clicks to my ear. The periscope screen — it was cracked, but not too badly — quite suddenly came alive with stars, with a dark globe upon the surface of which twinkled the lights of cities.

So far, not too bad.

I looked at the gyroscope controls. They were of the type to which I was accustomed — a transparent sphere in which swam a little model ship, its sharp stem almost touching the graduations within the transparency. The two control wheels were so designed as to be operable by one wearing space armour; even so, they were awkward. I turned the model through one hundred and eighty degrees, pressed the button, waited. Nothing happened. The reflected image of Carinthia still hung in the centre of the periscope screen.

"Ann," I said.

"Yes, Johnnie?"

"Hang on to something back there. I'm going to use the steering jets."

A few seconds later she reported, "All secure."

I stabbed another button. Nothing happened. I should, by this time, have been rather surprised if anything had happened. The failure of the ship to respond to her controls merely confirmed the evidence of the lightless control panels. A flying splinter from the transceiver must have sliced through, or almost through, the cable trunkway. The only circuit unbroken must be that of the periscope control.

So, I thought, periscope, one number. Accelerometer, ditto.

I stared at the simple, purely mechanical instrument — the spring, the pointer, the scale. It wasn't much more than nothing, but it was better than nothing.

"Anna," I said.

"Yes? I thought that you were going to use the steering jets. We're still waiting."

"I am going to use them, if your boyfriend can work them from his end to my orders. Ask him that, and ask him if he can do the same with the gyro."

There was a long pause, then, "He says that he can."

"Good."

But I shall have to breathe, I thought, and I don't know if the air in this suit will see us down. I raised my eyes, cricked my neck and read the gauge inside my helmet. What I saw was not comforting. So I unstrapped myself, went to the rack on which three suits kept in the control room were stretched. The suits were not undamaged but, to my intense relief, the air tanks of all three were unholed and at full pressure. I disconnected them, carried them to the chief officer's chair, where I used the safety belt to secure them. I strapped myself again into the captain's chair.

"Actuate gyro," I ordered.

"Actuate gyro." Then: "Gyro actuated."

"Swing ship at right angles to short axis."

"Swing ship at right angles to short axis."

I was not expecting to hear the familiar whine, but hear it I did, although faintly, the sound carried by the fabric of the ship and the fabric of my suit. The great globe ahead swung slowly away. Swung, and, at last, dipped below the ragged horizon of the buckled port frames. I didn't look at the stars that had replaced it but kept my attention on the periscope screen. After a long time the first sliver of almost intolerable light swam into view. I jabbed the polarizer control, was relieved when it functioned.

"Easy," I said. "Easy. . . ." Then: "Hold her!"

"Hold her!"

I adjusted the polarizer. "Anna," I said, "there's a sort

81

of green circle against the whiteness. Would that be Pilsen?"

"Yes. The gardens under the dome."

"And the spaceport?"

"Just to the north of the city. The red flashing beacon."

I made further adjustments, could just make out the tiny spark. It was well off-center on the screen.

"Actuate gyro," I ordered again. "Ship's head to port. . . . port. . . . Hold her!"

"Hold her."

I increased the periscope magnification, found another, smaller, green dome. I turned up the illumination of the graticules, rotated the scale until I had both domes against it. They were receding from each other steadily.

"Main venturi ready," I ordered.

"Main venturi ready."

"Set for one gravity."

"Set for one gravity. . . . All set."

"Fire!"

I wished that there were some means of controlling the volume of sound in the helmet phones, and hoped that Anna would not be so deafened by the noise level in the engine room as to be unable to hear my orders. I looked away from the screen to the little pointer of the accelerometer, saw it creep down to the numeral one. I looked back to the screen, saw that the recession of my two markers one from the other was almost halted.

"Cut drive!" I shouted.

I did not hear Anna's reply, but the screaming thunder abruptly ceased.

"Port steering jets, one-second blast!"

"Port steering jets, one-second blast!"

On the screen the Pilsen dome was now centered; the other dome was receding from it barely perceptibly. Gravitation: 0.3, I thought. Acceleration: 0.25? And what about lateral drift?

But before I did anything else it was necessary to ship a new air tank. I accomplished this without much trouble, although there was a moment of panic when at first the instantaneous coupling of the full tank refused to engage, then took a childish pleasure in throwing the almost empty tank out of the glassless viewport.

Even more childishly I wondered why it should be necessary to clutter up the control rooms of spaceships with all manner of electronic equipment.

Chapter Fifteen

FIVE HOURS and two air bottles later, I wasn't feeling so cocky. Just imagine that you're a juggler. Just imagine that your speciality is to balance a billiard cue on the tip of your nose, and an assortment of crockery on top of the cue. Just imagine that you are obliged to perform this feat not for five minutes, but for five hours. Just imagine that, to make things a little harder, your reaction time has been slowed down more than somewhat.

That's what it was like.

It wouldn't have been so bad if I'd been able to manipulate gyroscopes and steering jets directly from the control room. But every order had to be given verbally, and every order had to be given to Anna Bentz, who passed it on to the not very bright Nikki. I did think of having Nikki wear the suit so that I could give him his orders first-hand, but that would have meant that he would have had to handle his controls with heavily gloved hands. A spacesuit with detachable gloves or detachable helmet would have been the answer, but unluckily *Moonmaiden*'s spacesuits were inexpensive models, just good enough to pass the tests and no better.

Of all the instruments, it was the radar that I missed the

most badly. Without it, our jerky descent was a matter of guesswork — and, towards the finish, not very inspired guesswork. Ironically enough, it was the very lack of this navigational aid that had made a landing mandatory. With radar I could have flung the ship into a nice, stable orbit around Wenceslaus, there to hang until a tug could be despatched to do something about us. Without radar, to land was the lesser of several evils.

And radio would have been a blessing. Radio could have been a blessing if Port Pilsen Spaceport Control had dedigitated and decided to use the spacesuit frequency as soon as it became obvious that our main transceiver was dead. But they were a dim bunch and, I learned later, hunted up and down the wavebands until somebody had a long-overdue rush of brains to the head and thought that it was just possible that *Moonmaiden*'s people might be wearing spacesuits. By that time it was too late for Spaceport Control to be of any assistance to me. By that time the fresh voice yelping into the helmet phones was no more than an annoying nuisance.

An annoying nuisance?

A dangerous one.

"Port Pilsen to *Moonmaiden*. Port Pilsen to *Moonmaiden*. Do you hear me? Do you hear me? Over."

I ignored the query. "Anna, fire Numbers two and three steering jets. One-second blast."

"Fire two and three. One second."

"Port Pilsen to *Moonmaiden*. What was that? Over."

"Main drive — oh point three five G. . . ."

"Port Pilsen to *Moonmaiden*. What was that? Over."

"*Moonmaiden* to Port Pilsen. Shut up, damn you! Anna, Main drive — oh point two five."

"Port Pilsen to *Moonmaiden*. You are overshooting. You are overshooting. Correct your line of fall. Over."

I stared into the periscope screen with watering eyes. I could see the domed administration buildings, the high control tower. I could see the landing apron plainly enough, a circle of grey, almost black concrete against the silver dust. And I could see, too, that there were ships on the apron — a large one, presumably one of the Moon Ferries, and two smaller craft. Had the apron been clear I should have risked a landing on its hard surface. Had I been less exhausted I should still, I think, have risked a landing. But I just couldn't balance that wobbling billiard cue with its top load of crockery on the tip of my sweating nose any longer. The edge of the apron drifted to the edge of the periscope screen. I let it drift. It drifted off the screen. And, below us, the featureless dust looked close. It was close. I could see it flaring into incandescent flurries in the backblast of our main exhaust.

"Port Pilsen to *Moonmaiden*. Port Pilsen to *Moonmaiden*. You have overshot. Compensate. Compensate. Over."

"Main drive," I ordered, "oh point two. Number One steering jet, one second. Main drive, oh point on. . . . *Cut all!*"

"Cut all!" came Anna's reply.

"Port Pilsen to *Moonmaiden*. You —"

We fell.

We fell further than I had estimated that we should. I braced myself for the shock, but there was none. We fell, and we went on falling. When I saw the grey, powdery tide sweeping in over the port rims I realized what was happening.

Had there been nobody in the engine room, and had I been able to exercise direct control from the control room, I think I should have risked a blast on the main drive — after all, *Moonmaiden* wasn't my ship. But Anna was back there and, of course, Nikki. So the risk was out.

Had I been in better trim mentally and physically I should have been able to get my buckles unsnapped in time to have made an attempt at escape — and that would have been the very worst thing that I could have done. A ship buried deep in the dust, I learned later, is easy to locate; a man so buried is very lucky if he is located while there is still air in his tanks. As it was, I sat there, plucking feebly at the buckles, while the fine powder, almost fluid, poured in over the deck, up around my legs, to chest level, to and above helmet level.

"Port Control to *Moonmaiden*," said a voice oozing gloomy, I-told-you-so satisfaction. "You overshot."

"I know," I said.

"Johnnie!" Anna's voice was sharp. "Johnnie! Where are we? What's happened?"

"We're down," I told her. "Well down, and sinking deeper."

I stared at the greyness, dimly visible in the feeble illumination of the instrument lights inside my helmet, that was pressing against the transparency of my visor. I wondered what would happen if the visor should break; told myself, but not very convincingly, that on a world with relatively light gravitation, pressures would be correspondingly low.

A new voice came on the air, a voice that held the crispness of authority, a voice that conveyed the impression that its owner knew what he was talking about.

"Port Captain here, *Moonmaiden*. The rescue plant is on its way." There was a pause. Then: "Do you hear me, *Moonmaiden*?"

"I hear you."

"What happened? What's the situation on board?"

"Explosion," I said. "Control room wrecked. Captain, chief, and second officers, chief engineer — all dead."

"Who is that speaking?"

"John Petersen. Passenger."

"Who brought her in?"

"I did."

"What is the situation, Petersen? How many survivors? Where are they?"

"Three survivors. Purser and second engineer in engine room. Compartment airtight, but only one spacesuit there, and that with almost empty tanks. Myself in what's left of the control room, buried in this damned dust. Wearing suit. About half an hour's air left."

"Thank you. Stay where you are, all of you."

"I seem to have no option," I said, staring at the formless greyness.

"What compartment's holed?" asked the Port Captain.

"Control room. Officer's flat. At the moment there's vacuum in the axial shaft; we had to use it as an internal airlock."

"Good. Tell your engineer to repressurize the axial shaft."

I passed the order to Anna, heard her repeat it to the engineer. Then: "Anna," I asked, "what sort of rescue equipment do they have here?"

"I've seen it," she said. "It's always kept in a state of readiness. I've seen it, but I've never seen it used. It's like a huge tractor, with the body of a big, flat-bottomed boat. There's a sort of flexible tunnel, or trunk, that can be extended from its underside. . . ."

"I hope that it doesn't take too long," I said, looking up at the needle of the gauge inside my helmet. It was like the hand of a clock; a clock that was ticking away the remainder of my life. It was one of those utterly unimportant but utterly frustrating things that saved me from panic. There was an itch developing on the skin of the small of my back, an itch that normally, I could have relieved by somewhat complicated wrigglings inside my suit. But I couldn't wriggle. The pressure of the dust held me motionless. Whatever danger I was in became absolutely unimportant in comparison with that maddening discomfort.

"Port Captain to *Moonmaiden*. Directly over you — operating blaster."

I didn't know what the blaster was. I didn't like the sound of it. I was about to ask for details when, suddenly, there was light, blinding daylight, in which the fine dust swirled like dissipating mist. I looked up and saw a huge funnel overhead that, on the end of its trunk, looked like a waterspout or tornado. The funnel dipped and I could see, strapped inside its rim, a spacesuited figure, a man who held a long rod in both hands. The end of the rod touched the twisted metal of the port frames and there was a blue flare of electrical energy. The battered metal sagged and rent, was swept away by the same force that had dispelled the dust.

I unbuckled my belt, got unsteadily to my feet. Something seized me, tugged me, buffeted me, pulled and pushed me towards the edge of the now almost open platform that was the control room deck. A voice in my helmet phone bellowed, "Get back into your seat, you fool!"

I teetered there, almost falling overboard into the swirling dust sea, into the crater that was almost a whirlpool, on the edge of which I glimpsed a huge, ungainly construction from which snaked the long trunk. I teetered there, keeping my eyes fixed on the salvage ship, the one fixed point in a swirling unstable universe. Then, in desperation, I threw myself forward. I landed on my hands and knees, almost at once began to slide backwards, and clutched frantically at the shattered pedestal of the transceiver. I flattened myself on the deck and then, when I recovered my breath, started to crawl towards the chair that I had vacated. Dimly I noted that the man had dropped from the funnel and, with his rod, was clearing the deck of all obstructions.

I reached the chair, clung to it, then heard, transmitted through the steel flooring, a metallic clang. I looked up then, saw that the funnel had dropped, had enclosed a wide area of the control room, including the chairs and the hatch to the axial shaft. The rescue man was running the tip of his rod along the inner circumference of the funnel — welding this time, not burning or cutting.

I heard him ask somebody, "How does she look from up there?"

"Looks good, Joe," came the reply. "The dust's drifting back, but there's no sign of a blow. The seal's tight."

"Then reduce pressure." He turned to me, helped me to my feet. He said, "You can open your helmet now, if you wish."

I did so wish. The atmosphere inside the suit was hot and humid, and it stank. The air in the funnel held the taint of machinery, but it was clean. All that I wanted to do was just to breathe, and breathe. Without much interest I watched the stranger manipulating the manual controls of the airtight door, watched it slide to one side to reveal the deep well of the axial shaft, the deep well with the spiral staircase up which two figures were mounting slowly.

The man called Joe asked, "Is that all of you?"

"All," I said. "But there'll be some bodies in the officers' flat."

"You were lucky," he said. "It's a good job for you that we have regular rescue drills. It's years since the last ship was lost in the dust."

"I suppose we were lucky," I said.

I stooped to help Anna out of the hatch. She stood with me while the engineer, Nikki, emerged. He did not look at me with gratitude but with an expression that I realized, with a shock, was close to hatred. But, I thought, even though he's only a puddle-jumper, he's still a spaceman, and he'll be blaming me for almost having lost his ship. Almost? I didn't know how good the Port Pilsen rescue and salvage organization was. They had saved our lives, but could they save *Moonmaiden*?

Slowly the engineer began to clamber up the ladder inside the huge trunk. Anna squeezed my hand, the pressure registering even through our gloves, then followed him.

"Up you go," said the rescue man to me. "Up you go, skipper. We don't know yet if we can hold this cow, but if she goes, she'll go sudden!"

Up I went.

Chapter Sixteen

IT WAS all of a week before I was able to make a start on the business that had brought me to Wenceslaus. I was a witness — *the* witness, perhaps — at the official inquiry that was being held to look into the loss of *Moonmaiden*. Yes, the ship was a total loss. The cables holding her to the huge pontoons floating on the surface of the dust sea had parted and she had drifted down, down; down to the solid core of the satellite, and with her had gone the possibility of an expert examination of the wrecked control room.

I told my story, slightly censored.

Anna told her story, slightly censored.

(In view of this censorship, and in view of the slight suspicion that seemed to exist regarding our absolute truthfulness, we decided that it would be better if our unfinished business stayed that way.)

Nikki told his story.

As always is the case, there was a great deal of wisdom after the event displayed by people who weren't there. We should have done this, we should have done that. I should not have attempted to land, but should have adjusted trajectory so as to miss Wenceslaus, happy in the knowledge that a rescue tug would be sent as soon as it became apparent to Port Pilsen that something was seriously amiss. And so on, and so on. I hadn't quite been expecting a medal for my efforts but, even so, I was annoyed by the attitude of most of those at the inquiry, some of whom even succeeded in conveying the impression that Moon Ferries, Incorporated, were behaving with extreme kindness in not suing me for the value of their ship.

And then there were the expert witnesses, all of whom tried to shake my story of the control room's having been burst outwards. They seemed to find my account of the explosive transceiver especially ludicrous. One of them, the radio superintendent of Moon Ferries, told the court that the transceiver aboard *Moonmaiden* had been a new set, fitted that very trip, and had assured the judge that in the event of a sudden drop of control room pressure there would be no possibility whatsoever of the set's exploding.

Finally a theory was evolved to account for the tragedy. A tiny meteorite, the experts said it must have been. A tiny meteorite, of contraterrene matter. It was recommended that the Carinthian Survey Service make a thorough sweep of the volume of space enclosed by the Carinthian System for any similar navigational hazards. It was recommended that all ships of Carinthian registry be fitted with an emergency transceiver to be sited somewhere amidships. It was recommended that all future tonnage be built with a greater number of airtight divisions. The rescue squad was complimented on its smart work. I was complimented more on my luck than on my skill.

And that was that.

When the inquiry was over I went with Anna to the Spacemen's Hostel in which we had both been staying. I had time for one drink with her at the bar, a hasty one at that. She was returning to Carinthia immediately in *Moon Empress*. I walked with her to the airlock, then stood by the wide window watching her slim, spacesuited figure walking out to the shining tower that was the ship. I wondered, without much interest, if I should ever see her again.

I was aware that somebody was standing at my side. I turned, saw that it was Joe, the man to whose skill we owed our lives.

"Staying on, skipper?" he asked.

"Yes. On Wenceslaus, that is. I shall be moving out to Pilsen, though. I'm booked in at the Strauss-Hilton."

"Not a bad pub," he admitted. "Drink? We can watch the *Empress* shove off from the bar."

"It's a fine idea," I said.

We adjourned to the bar, watching the activity around the ferry rocket through the big window, sipping cold beer.

"Pity that judges have never been spacemen," said Joe. "The old bastard was rough on you."

"It's his job," I said.

"Talking of jobs," he said.

"Go on," I told him. "Finish whatever it was you were going to say."

He seemed embarrassed. "It's none of my business, skipper, but I did hear that you were here as some sort of detective, although how you can be one without an office full of apparatus beats me. But you know how things get around. . . ."

"I do," I said.

He looked around, making sure that we were alone. He even glared suspiciously at the robot bartender that had withdrawn on its rails to the far end of the counter and was humming quietly to itself.

"Go on," I said.

He whispered, "There are funny things going on here."

"Such as?"

"Sabotage."

That transceiver, I thought.

"We held her," he said. "We held her on the trunk, even though the crash wagon was starting to slide. Then we got the pontoons out, and the cables. We were all done in by that time, and she was secure, and we turned in. We should have left a guard, perhaps, but we didn't."

"I thought that a cable parted," I said.

"A cable did part," he told me. "But this is the point, skipper. I made sure that all cables were in the fairleads, that there was no chafe. But the story is that one cable was chafing on a sharp edge." He grunted. "It could have been, too — if somebody shifted it."

"Who'd do a thing like that?" I asked.

"You're the detective," he said.

"Am I?" I countered.

The warning siren put a stop to conversation — the siren that, although useless in the airlessness outside, was still sounded inside the administration buildings. We watched vehicles and personnel withdrawing from around the stern of the ship. We watched the first flickers of flame, pale, almost invisible in the bright sunlight. We watched the *Empress* lift, slowly at first, then with mounting acceleration.

Somebody turned the siren off.

"Did you report it?" I asked.

"Report what?"

"This business about the cables."

"Of course. I want to keep *my* jets clear, don't I? And that's the trouble. Everybody thinks that I've just made up the story to keep my jets clear. But they're all very decent about it. Mistakes can happen, and all the rest of it. In view of my past good record, blah, blah." He added, "A bloody expensive mistake."

"I'm glad that other people make mistakes of that kind," I said. "I got rather tired of being told about my bloody expensive mistake in the court."

"But it wasn't a mistake," he insisted. "The cables were all in the fairleads."

I drank with him for a while longer, then left him. His story of sabotage had convinced me. But why? Oh, I thought, it's obvious: With the ship gone, all evidence of the previous sabotage is gone. And surely, I told myself, a chemical explosive would have left some evidence.

I went to the telegraph office, made out a message to send to Steve Vynalek. I wrote it out on the form, then crumpled the form and thrust it into my pocket. Such a message — it was to ask that inquiries be made as to the origin of any new equipment fitted to *Moonmaiden* prior to her fatal voyage — would have to pass through far too many hands. Joe's story had made it plain that there were hostile interests on Wenceslaus. My queries could wait until I was in the Strauss-Hilton, until I had access to a private visiphone with scrambler attachment.

I returned to my room, completed my packing. I ordered a cab, then climbed into my spacesuit, the one that I had worn when I brought *Moonmaiden* in, the one that Moon Ferries had let me keep as a souvenir of the occasion. Now that it had been thoroughly deodorized I could feel a certain affection for it.

I carried my baggage down the main airlock. The cab was waiting inside the compartment. I looked at it curiously. It was like a flat-bottomed boat with a high, upsweeping prow. The driver and his passengers sat in a pressurized cabin that was a transparent bubble on top of the almost raftlike hull.

The driver got out of the cabin, looked at my suit with a certain disdain; he was wearing a sleeveless shirt, shorts and sandals. He said, "There's no need for that, mister. Betsy, here, doesn't leak. "She's as safe as a ship."

"That's what I'm afraid of," I said. "But if you feel that you must have conversation, I'll leave the visor up."

He grunted, slung my bags into the back of the cabin, waited for me to board, then slid into the driver's seat beside me. As the doors slid shut I saw the needle of the big pressure gauge of the airlock begin to drop. When it hit zero the airlock doors slid open.

"Strauss-Hilton?" asked the cabbie.

"That's right."

The cab began to move. The high prow of the thing hid what was happening ahead from view, but looking astern I could see a jet of dust shooting aft. It seemed to be an efficient enough means of transportation.

"Will you be here long?" asked the cabbie.

"I can't say."

"Came in on the *Empress*, did you?"

"No."

He searched for another conversational gambit. "You might find the Moon interesting. Long days here. The Moon keeps the same face turned to Carinthia all the time. But we work on the Carinthian clock and calendar. You'll get used to it."

"I already have," I told him.

"Yeah. Of course. You said that you didn't come in on the *Empress*." He peered at what little he could see of my face in the helmet rudely. "You came in on the *Maiden*," he cried triumphantly. "You're the fellow who brought her in."

"Yes."

"You must be popular," he said. "Yes, sir. You must be popular. One ship down in the dust. . . ."

"These things happen," I said.

"Not very often," he said.

"Once was enough for me," I said.

"Yeah. I'll bet it was." He drove in silence for a few minutes. Then: "This'll be your first time outside the spaceport, then."

"Yes."

"I'll swing Betsy so you can see Pilsen." The cab veered to the left. "There she is. The finest little city on Wenceslaus. The garden city."

I looked at the dome that was rearing up over the edge of the horizon, the dome that, even at this distance, seemed verdantly aglow with the green growing life inside it.

Chapter Seventeen

THERE WAS only a slight delay outside Pilsen while the cabbie talked to the lock-keeper on his radiophone. Then the big gates slid open and we drifted into the compartment, the cab sprouting small wheels as soon as we made the transition from dust to a solid flooring.

"Don't you ever get trouble with sand in the bearings?"

I asked.

"Nah, mister. The damned stuff's so fine that it's a lubricant."

The outer doors shut and the chamber was pressurized. The inner doors opened. We rolled into the city. I looked around with interest. I had been in moon cities before — on Earth's moon, on the Jovian and Saturnian satellites. They all followed the same general design: plain, unobtrusive architecture, vast areas of transparency opening on the splendid outside scenery. Here it was different. The architecture was almost fussy, and every street was, in effect, a splendid garden with trees and flowerbeds along the sidewalks. There was an occasional glimpse to be had of the sky through the interlaced foliage. Nowhere was there as much as a hint of the flat desolation outside.

"Kapek Circle," said the driver. "The Strauss-Hilton."

He drew to a stop outside a somewhat ornate building that overlooked the Circle, got out of the cab and unloaded my baggage, being careful to keep in on the mosaic footpath well clear of the grass plots. I thanked him and paid him. A man whom, at first glance, I took to be a galactic admiral saluted me and asked courteously, "You are giving us the honour of your patronage, sir?"

"Yes. Petersen's the name."

"This way, Captain Petersen."

Promotion, I thought. But I suppose I'm a pretty obvious spaceman.

The foyer of the hotel did more than follow the same pattern as the streets outside; it had improved upon it. I followed the admiral through the almost trackless jungle, fetched up at the reception desk. The girl on duty should have been wearing a fragment of leopard skin and a bright blossom in her hair. She was wearing a smart black business suit and a bright blossom in her hair. "Captain Peterson," said the admiral in introduction, then returned to his post of duty.

"Captain Petersen?" asked the girl, a little doubtfully.

"*Mr* Petersen."

"Oh, yes, Mr Petersen. We've put you in Room 37."

"A room with a view, I hope."

"*All* our rooms have views, Mr Petersen. Room 37 overlooks the Circle."

"Good. Visiphone, I suppose?"

"Of course."

"Scrambler?"

"One can be fitted, at a slight extra charge."

"Could you fit one as soon as possible? I shall be making some rather important business calls to New Prague."

"Certainly." She spoke briefly into some sort of intercom, then looked up and smiled. "It will be done within five minutes."

Service with a smile, I thought. I'm glad that it's Steve who's paying the bill here and not me. . . .

The girl gave me my key and a very young-looking commodore picked up my baggage, trotted with it to a clearing in the undergrowth where, almost hidden by luxuriant flowering creepers, were the doors of the lift shaft. We rode the cushion of compressed air to the third floor, walked the short distance along the corridor to my room. The door opened as we got there and an overalled mechanic came through it. He nodded to us briefly, said, "Scrambler fixed."

I thanked him, followed the commodore into the room. It looked comfortable enough, although the superabundance of potted plants gave it rather a greenhouse atmosphere. "Will that be all, sir?" asked the commodore as I tipped him.

"All," I said firmly.

Then, as he was leaving, I thought of something.

"Spy beams," I said.

"They're illegal here, sir," he said virtuously.

"I know. But I'd like a blocker."

"You'll have to ask the desk," he said. He went to the visiphone, punched a button. The screen lit up and the blonde in the black business suit looked out from it. "Gentleman in 37 would like a blocker," he said.

"Tell him that it will take thirty minutes to install," she said. "And there will be —"

"A slight extra charge," I finished.

She smiled sweetly. "However did you guess, Mr Petersen?"

"I'm taking a correspondence course with the Rhine Institute," I told her.

When the young commodore left me I got out of my spacesuit. Then I did some unpacking. I took from my briefcase the documents relating to Fergus and the photographs of him and his daughter. Then I started to put them back again, remembering that the blocker had yet to be installed. I laughed at myself and abandoned the secretive action. The plastic of the briefcase would no more block a spy beam than would the walls of the hotel. If anybody did have a beam on me he would have read, by this time, every paper in my possession. The blocker, however, would be of value when I made my call to Steve. It, together with the scrambler, would prove an impassable barrier to prying eyes and ears.

But where, I wondered, should I start? I looked at the photograph of Elspeth Fergus. She would make as good a starting point as any. She was so like Ilona. *Damn Ilona*, I thought. And then, I still had to maintain some sort of a front. There was this Kravik man, the allegedly erring husband. The first thing to do would be to go through the motions of putting some sort of tail on Kravik. That should not be hard; he was staying at the Strauss-Hilton.

There was a knock at the door.

The mechanic came in, carrying a square box. He dumped it on the carpet.

"First a scrambler," he grumbled. "Now this."

"It's all in a day's work," I told him.

"Not often it isn't," he grunted. "The last time was when we had the Shaara Ambassadress staying here. As though anybody would be interested in the sex life of a bunch of communistic bumblebees."

"Other bumblebees might be," I said.

I watched him plug the extension cord into a wall socket, then unlock the lid of the box. He opened it, revealed dials and switches. Mumbling to himself, he adjusted the controls. He growled, "She'll do."

"How do you know?"

"You just have to take my word for it, is all."

He snapped the lid shut, relocked it, shuffled out of the room.

When he was gone I went to the door and put the catch on the spring lock. Then I went to the visiphone, pressed the button for the switchboard. I told the girl that I wanted to make a call to New Prague. She told me that there would be a slight delay. I smoked a cigarette while I waited. I wished that I could be sure that the blocker was working, but I should soon be able to find out.

"You're through," I heard the girl say.

Steve's face looked at me from the screen. "John," he said. "We were worried about you, Liz and I."

"Scramble," I said.

Lines and colours dissolved into an abstract painting from which issued unintelligible sounds. I hoped that I had remembered correctly the combination that Steve had given me, twisted the dials on my own instrument to the proper sequence.

The screen cleared.

"Now what?" demanded Steve. "I suppose you realize that all this is costing money."

"It's cost plenty already, but we're not paying it. Lloyd's can afford it."

"Lloyd's? What do you mean?"

"Before we talk any further, would you mind putting your spy beam on to me? I'm at the Strauss-Hilton, as arranged. In Room 37."

"Okay," he said.

I smoked another cigarette.

Steve's face came back into the screen. He said, almost

accusingly. "You're using a blocker."

"I know. What I didn't know was if the damned thing was working. I know now. So we can talk. Listen, Steve, *Moonmaiden* was sabotaged. She was sabotaged twice: once in space, the second time after the landing. The cables were cut and she sank into this slippery dust of theirs, beyond recovery."

"Are you sure? I've already read the transcript of the inquiry proceedings, but there was no hint of sabotage."

"The so-called expert witnesses weren't there; I was. I'm pretty sure that there was a time bomb planted in the transceiver. I've found out that it was a new transceiver, installed that last time at Port Tauber. Can you make inquiries as to where that transceiver came from, who fitted it?"

"I will," he said. "But, Johnnie, you aren't all that important."

"I didn't think that I was, either. But somebody must think so."

"But to destroy a ship, and all her people, just to get rid of one man!"

"It's been done before," I said. "If you were any kind of a policeman you'd know about the cases."

"I know that it's been done before," he said tartly. "But that doesn't stop me from being shocked about it." He looked thoughtful. "I think that you'd better stay put, Johnnie. Meanwhile, I'll make a few investigations at this end. I'll call you back."

"All right," I said. "But what about this Kravik business? Hadn't I better maintain the front that we agreed upon at first?"

"Moon Ferries," he told me, "is a subsidiary of your old outfit, T.G. Clippers. They use T.G. Clippers' repair facilities and draw certain items of equipment from the T.G. stores at Port Tauber. The transceiver was installed by T.G. technicians. The technician who installed the thing has been transferred to Port Oberth, on Silesia."

"And the rest?" I asked. I could see that he had by no means run dry.

"The rest?" There was a puzzled grin on his face. "Well, it looks as though all of us are barking up the wrong tree. It looks as though Fergus *is* tinkering with time, but it looks as though he's found some way of seeing into the future."

"That's what I've been thinking," I told him. "But what's made you think it?"

"Just that Elspeth Fergus put through a call to Port Tauber days before we'd decided to send you to the Moon, asking to be notified when a Mr John Petersen booked passage for Wenceslaus."

"Odd," I said.

"Odd," he agreed.

"About Kravik —" I began.

"Go through the motions," he told me. "After all, we don't know how much the other side knows. We don't know what they know. We don't know who they are, even."

"Right."

"I'll be coming out to the Moon," he said. "As soon as I can."

"And how soon will that be?"

He shrugged. "It'll be all of ten days. With one of the three ships off service. . . ."

"Permanently," I added.

"Yes. Permanently. Just you try to keep yourself in service, Johnnie, until I get there."

"I'll try," I said.

"Good. See you."

"See you," I said.

Chapter Eighteen

I LOCKED all my papers, with the exception of Kravik's photograph, into my briefcase, stowed the briefcase into one of my suitcases and locked that. Locks and keys, I know, exist only to inconvenience honest men, but I thought that I'd better go through the motions of maintaining secrecy. I twirled the combination dial of the visiphone scanner, wiping out the setting. Then, sitting down again, I carefully studied the little likeness of my quarry — or my simulated quarry. I wasn't quite sure how to set about finding him; to make inquiries at the desk might be a little too obvious. But did that matter?

In any case, I felt that a drink was indicated before dinner.

I left my room, walked along the corridor with its vine-covered walls, then down a stairway that tried, not to unsuccessfully, to imitate a mountain path on a well-forested slope. I was relieved to find that the bar was severely functional, a place where it was not intended that the serious drinkers should be distracted by the exotic flora of a score of planets. The large room was almost full, although not crowded, cheerful.

I found a stool at the long counter, caught the eye of the lissome redhead who was serving. She flowed towards me. I ordered beer. It came in a pewter tankard. I like beer out of pewter, especially on low-gravity worlds. The heavy metal gives one's drink a feeling of weight.

After I had slaked my thirst I looked around me.

If the devil cast his net here, I thought, he'd get a fine haul of executives of assorted ages and sexes. Such as, for example, friend Kravik.

I had recognized Kravik almost at once. He seemed a little fatter than the photograph had depicted him, a little balder. He was sitting at a table with a slimly elegant, blondely expensive woman. He had eyes only for her, and

I can't say that I blamed him. I wondered if Steve Vynalek knew that my phony assignment was not so phony. I was rather glad that the assignment was a phony one; it looked as though Kravik would find himself in plenty of hot water without my aid.

I drained my tankard, ordered a fresh one. When it came I carried my drink to the empty table next to the one at which Kravik and his friend were seated, sat down, my back to the man and woman, my ears figuratively flapping.

She was saying, "You haven't seen the post office yet, Josef."

"Do they send telegrams by grapevine?" he asked, laughing.

She laughed in reply, then said, "Don't be silly. The post office is one of our sights here. It's better after sundown, of course, but sundown won't be for another four days. And if you see it first by daylight you get a better idea of what's going on."

"It will make a change," he said, "from trees and flowers and bushes and creepers and —"

"We are proud of our gardens," she told him.

"There is one fair flower of which Pilsen may justly be proud," he told her.

I was rather sorry that I hadn't switched on my wrist tape recorder.

"The coach leaves in fifteen minutes," she said.

"All right, darling. I'll just finish my drink."

I finished mine, gulping the remainder of the beer rather too hastily for comfort. I turned slightly in my chair to watch Kravik and his woman walk to the door; like a bear keeping company with a gazelle, I thought. I got to my feet and followed them, trying not to make it too obvious.

Outside the hotel they turned to the right. Tailing them was easier now, I could keep several other people between them and myself. They walked briskly, heading for a sign that jutted over the sidewalk reading: MOON TOURS. Set back from the footpath was a coach station, and there was another sign: POST OFFICE FIRINGS. COACH DEPARTS 1915 NPST. FARE $1.50.

Post Office firings? The ceremonial sacking of unsatisfactory staff? "Miss Bloggs, this package is distinctly marked FRAGILE, and yet you failed to drop it even once." "Miss Whatsit, this letter is stamped URGENT and you deliberately went out of your way to accord it priority . . ." And what would follow? The ritual branding of the offenders with cancellation stamps?

I bought a ticket at the desk, walked to the coach which Kravik and the blonde had already boarded. It was, I saw, of the conventional local design — the hull of a flat-bottomed boat with a transparent, pressurized cabin as superstructure, and little retractable wheels. There was, I noticed, a funnel-shaped aperture in the high prow — the intake? — and a venturi of sorts aft.

The coach was almost full; the only vacant seat was behind Kravik and the woman. I slid into it, hoping that the Goddess of Luck would look upon me as kindly when I started the real detective work. I looked at my fellow passengers. None of them was worthy of a second glance. The only interesting woman in the vehicle was the one sitting just ahead of me.

The driver climbed into his seat. The doors slid shut. The coach rolled silently out of the station, into the street. It was like driving through a huge conservatory. I heard the blonde babbling about Vegan fire trees and Aldebaran singing vines and all the rest of them; evidently she was a keen horticulturist. It seemed to be a national failing on Wenceslaus. Or perhaps that failing was confined to Pilsen? Perhaps other cities on this barren Moon had other things to offer. Such as, for example, improved post office firings. . . .

We came to one of the city airlocks, passed through it with hardly any delay. The wheels of the coach were withdrawn into their recesses; we skimmed out over the dust plain. The intolerably bright, slowly westering sun was almost ahead. The driver polarized the transparent dome.

I could see, far off, towers against the sky, a welcome break in the monotony of that otherwise featureless horizon.

The driver, once we were clear of the city, began talking softly into the microphone, delivering a nonstop monologue. Most of its subject matter I already knew. Most of it was dry-as-dust statistics of the kind that I had already extracted from the book that Anna had loaned me aboard *Moonmaiden*. And then he came up with a few new facts — or opinions. Wenceslaus, he declared, possessed the finest postal service in the known universe. Could be, I thought. Could be. If erring employees are dismissed in circumstances of public ignominy it will, I suppose, encourage the others. . . .

The towers, suddenly, it seemed, were nearer, were near.

There were towers, and there was a circle of dark-grey concrete on which were vehicles, scarlet painted dustsleds similar to the one in which we rode. There were clusters of spacesuited men, doing something to a rank of odd-looking tripods.

Whipping posts? I wondered.

"The mail for Brno is now being loaded," said our driver. "It has been weighed, and the solid propellant charge has been adjusted accordingly."

"Won't the rocket make a mess of the Brno launching pad when it lands?" asked Kravik.

"It would," said the driver, "if it hit the pad. But the charge has been so calculated that it will fall ten meters clear of the pad. The parachute at the tail of the rocket will prevent it from sinking into the dust."

"But won't the parachute hinder the flight of the rocket?" asked an earnest little man.

"The rocket," said the driver severely, "is being fired in a vacuum."

"But suppose the parachute tears off when the rocket hits the dust?" persisted the little man.

"There is a net under the dust, moored to pontoons."

There was a flash of orange flame, a puff of swiftly thinning white smoke, and the first rocket was gone. There was more activity on the launching pad, another flash of flame, and the second rocket was away. Then the third, then the fourth . . . I found the spectacle interesting, so much so that I borrowed a pair of binoculars from the little man across the aisle who, for some reason, was not using the intruments.

When I got them focused I found that I was looking at a group of officials who were taking no active part in the firings. One of them was a tall man dressed in what looked like a very expensive suit with a goldfish-bowl helmet. There was something familiar about what I could see of his features. He turned to face me.

It was Maleter, New Prague Branch Manager of Trans-Galactic Clippers.

Iron Man Maleter.

Chapter Nineteen

ON THE RUN back to Pilsen I lost interest in Kravik and his girlfriend. I was too busy marshalling facts, adding two and two and coming up with what seemed a quite probable five. Damn it all, I was supposed to be a detective, wasn't I? I was supposed to be able to make deductions without a skyscraper full of apparatus to help me, wasn't I? I was supposed to be able to carry out Mr Holmes's injunction to see *and* to observe. I was supposed to be able to use M. Poirot's "little grey cells".

All right.

1) *Moonmaiden* was sabotaged.

2) The sabotage had been carried out by means of a

time bomb, same having been placed in the transceiver.

3) The transceiver was from Trans-Galactic Clipper stores and had been installed by a Trans-Galactic technician.

4) Maleter was Carinthian Branch Manager of Trans-Galactic Clippers.

5) Maleter was on Wenceslaus.

6) ????

Was Maleter behind the sabotage? It looked that way, especially since the technician responsible for the installation of the new equipment had been transferred away from any possible interrogation. I wondered if the technician ever got as far as Silesia. I wondered if he would survive long if he did get that far. With a sudden chill I began to speculate upon my own chances of survival. Suppose, for example, there was a time bomb hidden in this coach? With the hull holed, the vehicle would sink swiftly under the dust, just as *Moonmaiden* had done. But it had been quite by chance that I had decided to witness the post office firings, whereas booking one's passage on any sort of interplanetary ship, even a moon ferry, is a fairly long drawn-out procedure.

Why should I be important?

But what was behind it all?

All right, I was investigating Fergus. Or I should be, once I got started. But I wasn't the first to investigate Fergus. Central Intelligence had been investigating him. The unnamed "powerful interests" had been investigating him. Powerful interests? Trans-Galactic Clippers? Holiday cruises to ancient Greece? Excursions to Rome, to see the Games? (Bring your own lions. . . .) But I had already decided that the time travel angle was the wrong one. Precognition, yes; time travel, no.

So . . . .

Suddenly the coach lurched, a woman screamed.

My eyes snapped open and I saw, directly ahead of us, a pillar of dust, a ragged column that slowly tumbled about itself. We slowed to a halt just short of it, slowed and stopped. We watched, in silence, the sliding, settling, flattening mound.

"The bloody fools!" swore the driver. "The bloody, bloody fools!"

The face he turned to us was whiter than the desert outside.

"What was it?" asked Kravik.

"Those copulating postmen, that's what it was. Those copulating postmen and one of their copulating rockets." He turned a switch on the panel of his transceiver. "Tourist coach here, calling post office. What in festering hell do you think you're playing at?"

"Post office . . ." came a faint, shaken voice. "Post office. . . . Did — did it miss?"

"Of course it bloody well missed! Do you think I'd be yapping to you if it hadn't? It missed all right — by the thickness of a whisker!"

". . . unfortunate accident . . ." I heard. ". . . apologies."

"And compensation!" roared the driver ". . . the necessary forms . . ." babbled the voice from the post office.

"Yes, we'll fill in your bloody forms! We'll fill you in, too, if we lay our hands on you!"

"It was an accident. Most unfortunate. . . ."

"Most fortunate," corrected our driver, a little calmer. "Most fortunate for you that it did miss."

"And for us," said Kravik dryly.

"You'll hear from us," growled the driver ominously, snapping off his set. He turned to face his passengers. "When we get back to Pilsen," he said, "I shall want the names and addresses of all you people. My company will bring suit on behalf of all of you."

The coach restarted. It seemed that everybody was talking at once. If the incident had done nothing else, it had broken the ice. I agreed with all that was being said. Yes, wasn't it simply *criminal*? Yes, hadn't we been lucky? Yes, just a small puncture in the pressurized cabin, and we'd be . . . .

Meanwhile, *had* it been an accident?

If not, how had Maleter known that I was aboard the coach?

The tailer tailed?

Could I have been followed, just as I had followed Kravik and his blonde?

I could, I decided.

Then a telephone call to the post office which Maleter was visiting as an official guest?

Why not? I asked myself.

And the important guest being allowed to play under strict supervision, of course — with one of the rockets. . . . And the accidental tripping of a firing switch. . . .

Even so, it was nice rocketry. Somebody must have calculated the charge. Somebody must have laid and trained the rocket launcher, somebody with experience as a combat rocketeer.

And why not?

For all I knew, all the rocket launching crew might be ex-Marines. Even though Carinthia was no longer a full member of the Federation her citizens had been eligible for service in the Federation's forces until quite recently, and some of them could have seen action.

We drifted into the airlock, experienced the usual short delay, then rolled through the streets of the city. I found that I was approaching all the greenery rather more than I had done before; it was so alive, it was in such contrast to the dessicated dust that, for the second time, had so nearly claimed me.

We turned into the coach station. The driver was first out and ran into the office. He emerged with a second man, carrying a light table on which was a stack of forms. He shouted, "Ladies and gentlemen, before you go, please leave your names and addresses."

We disembarked, formed into a line. I was just ahead of Kravik. He was looking over my shoulder as I wrote my name on the form. He said, "So you're Petersen. We must have a drink together when we get back to the hotel."

"Thanks." I told him, "but I'm beginning to think that people will be safer keeping well clear of me."

"Are you accident prone?" asked the blonde. "But this is fascinating. You must tell us all about it."

"Natalya," said Kravik, not without pride, "is a statistician. With the Outworld Insurance Corporation."

"The figures she deals with will not be as pretty as hers," I said gallantly. "But, seriously, I think you'd better stay away from me."

Kravik caught my arm, held me while the girl filled in her form.

"We're having that drink first," he said. "Come on, Natalya, we'll escort our friend back to the pub."

"You remember that I was telling you about Steve," went on Kravik. "Young Petersen is one of his friends."

"Petersen?" repeated the blonde. "Oh, yes, I remember now. You brought the *Moonmaiden* in. And what are you doing on Wenceslaus. Mr Petersen?"

"Watching me!" exploded Kravik, with a roar of laughter.

We walked back to the Strauss-Hilton together, but I never got that drink. As soon as we entered the foyer, I was accosted by the galactic admiral.

"Mr Petersen, sir," he said. "There's a young lady waiting to see you. She's in the lounge."

"Que custodiet custodien?" asked Kravik.

Chapter Twenty

SOFT MOSS underfoot and an intricacy of trunk and branch and vine, blossom and foliage, all around and overhead, and the slanting, golden rays of the afternoon sun — how reflected? how refracted? — and the melodious tinkle of falling water somewhere in the background and the girl, long, lovely limbs palely luminous in the green shadows, rising gracefully to her feet to greet me. . . .

For a long crazy moment I thought it was Ilona.

"Mr Petersen?" she asked, and the spell was broken.

Her voice was not the same, had not the same depth and huskiness, and the eyes, looking steadily into mine, were grey rather than blue, and her hair was not darkly brunette with coppery highlights, but red-gold. Yet the facial contours were there, and the bodily contours, although she carried herself with a coltish grace rather than with a studied elegance.

The spell was broken, but . . .

"Mr Petersen?" she repeated.

"Guilty," I admitted. "Miss Fergus?"

"Yes," she said. She went on, "I hope you don't mind my meeting you here. This is my favourite spot in Pilsen. It reminds me of Caribbea, of the gardens of our home there." She paused for breath. "My father and I spent many happy years on Caribbea."

"I know," I said.

"How do you . . .?" Then, with the beginnings of a puzzled smile, "But I suppose that you would know."

A waiter hurried by, incongruous in his harsh black and starched white, bearing a tray of drinks. I realized then that we were not alone in the enchanted forest. I glared at the other people, willing them to go away.

They did not.

"You wished to see me, Miss Fergus?" I asked inanely.

"But yes. My father. . . ."

I looked around me, studying the faces of those men at the nearby tables.

She said, "He's not with me. He's at the dome. He told me to —"

I put a hand out and grasped her upper arm. I felt a tingling shock at the queer familiarity of her skin.

"Not here," I said.

Her eyes widened in amazement, and then I saw understanding on her face. She was feeling, as I was feeling, that this arboreal lounge, with its cunningly disposed and maintained greenery, although still a glade in an enchanted forest, was one in which the enchantment had turned evil. She was beginning to fear, as I was fearing, what might be lurking in the shadows.

We walked slowly from the room and then up the stairs to the third floor, my free hand ready to snatch the pistol from its shoulder holster. We said nothing further until we were in my room, the door locked and bolted. She murmured, seeing the black, ugly box, "A blocker."

"Yes," I said. "If it's still working."

I went to the visiphone and put through a call to Steve Vynalek in New Prague, actuating the scrambler while I was waiting for it to come through. There was a long delay while the screen swirled with formless blobs of colour, while the speaker gabbled unintelligbly. Then the scrambler at the other end was switched on and the face of Steve's receptionist looked out at me.

"Mr Petersen," she said.

"Yes. I'd like to talk to Mr Vynalek."

Her face, already worried, became more so.

"He's — He's in hospital."

"In hospital?"

"Yes. There was a copter accident. At least, it was meant to look like an accident. But Steve was an excellent pilot, very careful. And rotor shafts just don't snap in midair."

"Is it serious?"

"Yes, it is. But he'll live, and be very little the worse for it." Pride almost replaced the worry. "He's tough."

"Good. But before we go any further, will you see if my blocker is working? You know how to handle the spy beam, don't you?"

She did, and I told her where to focus it. She left the visiphone and came back a minute or so later, assured me that the room was effectively blocked. I asked her for the details of the alleged accident and she told me as much as she knew. She told me that Central Intelligence was making investigations. She told me, too, that Steve had told her to tell me that I had better abandon the case.

"Not bloody likely," I said. "Things are just getting interesting. When you see Steve again you can tell him there have already been two attempts to rub me out. The *Moonmaiden* affair was the first — you'll already have heard about that. The second one was an hour or so ago. A mail rocket was fired accidentally and almost hit the dustsled in which I was riding."

"Then you should abandon," she told me, "and return to Carinthia."

"I haven't finished yet. I've made contact with Miss Fergus. Her father wants me out at his dome."

"That place is a young fortress," she told me. "You might be safer there, at that. But be careful."

"I will. And I'll report later what happens."

"Everything?" she asked with an odd emphasis, and I realized that Elspeth had moved within the scope of the scanner.

"Just tell Steve that I'm on the ball," I said.

"Will do. And good luck."

We switched off and I wiped out the scrambler setting.

Elspeth Fergus said, "I'm sorry, but I couldn't help overhearing. What was all that about Central Intelligence?"

"But surely you know what I'm here for," I said.

"I don't," she insisted. "All I know is that my father thinks that you're somehow important, that he has had me make inquiries about you. Weeks ago I was trying to find out when you were due on Wenceslaus."

"And when a member of the Fergus family starts making inquiries about somebody," I said, "other people get the idea that he's important."

"My father thinks," she went on, "that your destiny is somehow tied up with his."

"With *his*?" I asked.

There was a long silence.

"But I feel —" she said.

"When I first saw you . . ." I started to say.

"I know that it sounds crazy . . ." she said.

There was another long silence and the building up of tension, that tension that can be broken only one way. But there was a minor ritual to be observed, the pouring out of a small libation to those gods concerned with the management of human affairs. I went to the refrigerator — it had been stocked by the hotel as part of its much advertised service — and took out a bottle of champagne. And then I found that I was looking at it doubtfully. It may have been imagination, but there seemed to be something subtly wrong with the gold foil about the cork. I put the bottle back into the refrigerator.

She asked, with an attempt at lightness, "Don't I rate a drink?"

"You do," I assured her. "But not from *that* bottle."

"Is it something special, for someone special?"

"I think so. And I think the someone special is me."

"Pig," she said.

"You overheard the visiphone conversation," I told her. "You heard me say that there have already been two attempts on my life. This, I think, is the third."

She paled suddenly. She whispered, "I never thought that they would go so far."

"They?"

"We've known," she said, "that someone has been prying."

"Who are *they*?" I demanded.

"I don't know. But I think my father guesses."

"Maleter," I said softly. "Maleter. . . . Does that name mean anything to you?"

She looked thoughtful. "There was a Maleter," she said, "on Si Kiang, in Flammarion's Cluster. Iron Man Maleter, he was called. But he was killed, I think, in the revolution."

"You think?"

"I was a small girl," she said, "when we were on Si Kiang."

"Maleter . . ." I said again.

"But what do we do?" she asked.

"I should let you go back to your father's dome by yourself," I said. "But I don't think that it's me that they're really after. They've got the idea that I'm somehow important to him, so they want me out of the way. But you're important to him too."

"This is the first time that I've been outside the dome," she said, "since we became aware that we were being . . . investigated."

"And your father let you come without protection," I said.

Her slender hand flashed to the pocket of her shorts and I found myself looking into the muzzle of a deadly little Minetti automatic.

"Not quite without protection," she assured me. "Besides, he was quite sure that I should be returning. With you."

"How was he so sure?"

"That you will learn," she told me, "out at the dome."

Again there was the silence, the building up of tension. I heard the thud as her weapon dropped to the carpet. And then, quite suddenly, she was very close to me and her mouth was on mine and felt as though it belonged there, had always belonged there. My pistol, in its shoulder holster, was an uncomfortable, awkward pressure that had to be shed, and there were other pressures, other confinements, equally irksome, too much between us that had to be gotten rid of, and quickly, and then the softness of her was against me, the firm, resilient softness, and it was all so absolutely right, as it had been before and would be again . . . .

I looked at her in the dim light as she lay beside me on the bed, at the slender, lovely length of her, the unashamed beauty. Women I had known before, but no woman as I had know her. *(But Ilona?)* And yet this had been the first time.

The first time?

". . . like coming home," she murmured.

"So you feel it too?"

"And you?"

"And I."

She said, "This had to happen."

"Yes."

"It was . . . strange."

"No. Not strange. Not strange at all."

"I mean, it was strange how it wasn't strange."

She laughed. "Johnnie, you're as woolly as father is at times with his weird theories."

I wished that she hadn't mentioned her father. For a short time, for too short a time, my mission had been forgotten. For a short time there had been no need to hunt any further for any truth; all that was true in the galaxy had been contained by the four walls of this characterless room. And now I had been reminded of my real reason for being on Wenceslaus.

My real reason?

I told myself that my real reason had already been discovered, but I wasn't able quite to convince myself.

Chapter Twenty-one

ELSPETH'S SLED, she told me, was parked outside the hotel.

After I had packed I rang for a bellhop and we followed the lad down the stairs to the reception desk, where I paid my bill. It seemed a large one, especially since I had never spent a night or eaten a meal in the place. Presumably I was being charged for, among other things, the luxuries with which the refrigerator had been stacked. I wondered what would happen to that dubious bottle of wine. Perhaps I should have opened it and disposed of its contents in the toilet. But it was too late to worry about that. In any case, whoever was in charge of the supply of food and drink to the bedrooms would know whether or not any of it was poisoned, or drugged.

We went outside.

The galactic admiral saluted smartly and said to Elspeth, "Nobody has been near your sled, Miss Fergus."

"Thank you," she said.

I hoped that the admiral had not been neglecting his duty. I hoped that he was not in the pay of the opposition. But Fergus, according to his daughter, had been certain that she and I would return to his dome safely, and all the evidence seemed to indicate that he could and did foretell the future with considerable accuracy.

She got into the vehicle. I waited until the bellhop had stowed my baggage in the back, tipped the boy and followed her. I hoped that it would not be too far to the Fergus dome. It was a long time since I had eaten and all that had happened since my last meal had done nothing to decrease my hunger.

Silently we rolled through the avenues. Neither of us spoke; there was no need for speech. We were with each other. We were with each other again. . . . *Again?* I wondered why I should be thinking of this passion that had flared up between us as something that was being resumed after a long time. I wondered why I was bothering to wonder about it; told myself that sufficient unto the day was the beauty and wonder thereof.

Silently we rolled through the avenues, slid gently into one of the city airlocks. Elspeth waited until the inner doors were shut and then spoke softly into the microphone of the transceiver. "Please delay depressurization," she said, "until we are suited."

We got out of the sled. I pulled her suit from its rack at the back of the vehicle, helped her into it, not without reluctance. But something of the essential grace of her showed even through the tough, baggy plastic. I checked her air gauge, saw that her tanks were full. I took my own suit from where it had been placed on top of my baggage, put it on. I asked her, "Expecting any trouble?"

"Yes," she said soberly. "At least, I think so. Something seemed to tell me that we'd better be prepared."

There was, I thought, altogether too much crystal-gazing about this business. And I realized that I was not as fully prepared as I might be. Cursing myself, I got out of my suit again, removed my automatic from its shoulder holster. I pulled one of my suitcases out of the sled, practically unpacked it before I found the belt and the side holster. I put on the suit again, buckled the belt around my waist, holstered the pistol. I saw Elspeth grin, and then she was out of her suit and was removing the little pistol from the pocket of her shorts.

A voice said from the wall speaker: "Carrying weapons is illegal on this world. I must hold you in the airlock until the arrival of a police officer."

There was a permit in my wallet, issued on Carinthia but valid on Wenceslaus. I sighed at the thought of having to undress again to get at the little oblong of laminated plastic. But Elspeth saved me the trouble.

She said, "I am Miss Fergus. My father has permits for firearms for himself and all members of his family and staff. Please ring police headquarters to confirm this."

We took advantage of the wait to enjoy a cigarette. Then the voice of the lock-keeper said, "I must apologize for the delay, Miss Fergus. You may proceed."

We got back into the sled. Elspeth put her Minetti into the glove compartment. I asked her, "Can you use it?"

She said, "I can. And if you're observant you will have noted that the trigger action has been modified so that it can be used wearing spacesuit gloves."

"So I see. A neat job."

"Father is a clever engineer," she told me.

The outer doors slid open. Our motor whined. We rolled out onto the smooth dust and then, our wheels retracting, slid forward. I looked ahead, to port and starboard, saw only the grey, featureless plain. I looked astern, and with the speed of our passage away from it the great dome of Pilsen seemed to be foundering in the dust sea.

Elspeth made adjustments to the sled's transceiver, spoke briefly into the microphone. "Elspeth here, father. I have him with me. We're on our way now."

A man's voice replied. It was as I had expected it to sound: rather high-pitched, faintly querulous. "That's good, my dear. But be careful. I know that you'll get here, but be careful."

"We are being just that," she assured him, and switched off.

I said, "This fortune-telling must be a fairly short-range sort of affair."

She snapped, "It's not fortune-telling, Johnnie."

Rather hurt, I asked, "Then what is it?"

She said, "It's too complicated to tell you now. You'll have to see what it's all about when we get out to the dome."

For a while she concentrated on her driving, watching the little dial of the gyro compass. Or was it, I asked myself a directional gyroscope? Rotation of a planetary body is necessary before a gyroscope can become a compass. Wenceslaus rotated on its axis once every thirty Carinthian days, keeping always the same face turned to its primary. With such a slow period, would a gyrocompass work? For some foolish reason it seemed better to try to make mental calculations than to ask.

Suddenly I stiffened.

A black speck had appeared on the horizon to starboard, a black speck that increased in size as I watched it. I looked astern. Pilsen was now out of sight but there was another of the blacks there. I looed to port, and the

119

glaring sun was low now, low and blinding. I asked Elspeth to polarize the transparent bubble of the cabin. She looked at me, her face suddenly apprehensive behind the open visor of her helmet, did so. Yes, there was a third speck there, with a long dust trail behind it. Dust? But dust, in this near-vacuum, would fall almost immediately, just as our own trail was falling. Smoke? Yes, smoke it was; smoke, and a bright spark of fire.

I told Elspeth what I had seen.

She said quietly, "Rocket sleds. There are a few on Wenceslaus. They're faster than these ionized dust jobs, although their range is limited."

"Who owns them?"

"The police," she said doubtfully. "The post office."

"The post office," I repeated. "I've rather gained the impression, my dear, that on this satellite the post office is somebody's private army."

"You don't think . . . ?"

"I do," I said.

The speeding vehicles to port and to starboard were closing now. The one to starboard, the one that was reflecting the almost level rays of the sun, shone brightly scarlet. There was no doubt as to its ownership, although it had yet to make a hostile move. After all, I thought, it and its two companions could be mail vans making a routine run, carrying consignments of parcel mail or whatever sort of mail it was that was carried on the surface instead of being shot to its destination by rocket.

"There are no cities in this direction," said Elspeth.

The dust ahead of us erupted in a sudden flurry and I could see the bright sparks of tracers swimming towards us from the rocket sled to starboard. Elspeth put her wheel over, flung us in a tight turn to port. I told her sharply to shut her visor, saw her nudge with her chin the button that sealed her helmet. I did the same to mine, switched on my suit radio.

Somebody was saying, "Calling Petersen and Fergus. Calling Petersen and Fergus. Stop at once."

Our sled was still coming round in its tight turn, and then Elspeth straightened out, putting us on a course that would bring us close under the stern of the rocket sled that had been doing the firing. The sled that had been closing us to port opened fire but ceased almost immediately; the tracer bullets were hitting the dust too near to the other. The one that had been astern was coming up fast on our starboard hand.

If we could use the transceiver, I thought, we could call for help. I wasn't proud and, as far as I was concerned, postmen running amuck in rocket sleds armed with machine guns were a matter for police action. I opened my visor again, reached for the microphone, switched on the set. "Calling Port Pilsen Police," I shouted. "Calling Port Pilsen Police." From the speaker came a loud, continuous squealing. It was obvious that our adversaries had thought of everything and were jamming our signals.

I shut my helmet again. I saw the backblast of the sled under whose stern we were skimming bathe the side of our cabin with fire, but momentarily. Even so, it had been too close for comfort. I heard the strange voice in my helmet phones again, "Stop at once. Stop at once." There were more bright sparks of tracers flying about us and then, even through my helmet, I heard the thin, high scream of escaping air.

What followed was so confused that even now I find it hard to work out just exactly what did happen. The mail sleds had the advantage of superior speed, to say nothing of armament. Our advantage was that of superior manoeuvrability. The intention of the postmen was obvious enough: to enclose us in a circle around the rim of which would run their fast vehicles, then to destroy our motor with their machine gun fire. I don't think that they wanted to kill us — or, perhaps, it was just Elspeth whom they wanted alive rather than dead — and this policy must have hampered them.

What hampered them still more was the girl's superlative skill. Time and time again she evaded collision by the thickness of a coat of paint, time and time again bluffing her way through, forcing one of the scarlet sleds to give way. And I foolishly wasted time trying to get the windows of our cabin open. They had been buckled by the blast of heat from the rocket exhaust of the sled under the stern of which we had passed too closely.

I realized at last that if bullets could come through, then bullets could also go out. Then I tried to fire as I had been taught during my Reserve training: slowly, carefully, taking aim. At last, my mood compounded of exasperation and desperation, I loosed off a full clip at the two spacesuited figures in the nearest sled, one of them hunched over the controls, the other one in the act of bringing the mounted machine gun to bear on the stern of our own vehicle.

I missed them, of course — Elspeth at that moment made yet another of her tight turns. I missed them, but must have hit instead the tank of rocket fuel. There was a sudden gushing of blue flame, a short lived volcano into which one of the other sleds ploughed. I saw a blazing figure stagger out onto the surface of the dust — the surface that was still almost smooth in spite of all our manoeuvrings, the surface that was marked only by faint, fading ripples. I saw the burning man sink to his knees, to his waist, and then vanish, and saw the wreckage of the two sleds follow him. The third sled stopped, and weighted lines were thrown out of its open windows. Magnetic grapples? We didn't ask, and we didn't wait to see what happened. Elspeth put us on course again and we resumed our journey.

The last of the enemy sleds was out of sight and the gleaming dome of the Fergus laboratory had lifted over the horizon when our motor coughed and stopped, when we realized that a grey tide of the fine dust was rising slowly over our feet.

"Holed," I said unnecessarily. "We can plug the holes."

"We can't." said Elspeth. Her voice brightened. "But, as I told you, we shall get to the dome."

She scrambled out of her seat, reached into the compartment from which I had taken her spacesuit. She pulled from it two parts of odd-looking contraptions, slightly curved, boat-shaped affairs of plastic, each with straps on the concave sides. Perched on the back of her seat, her feet clear of the encroaching dust, she strapped one of the things on to each foot. Then, as I had done earlier, she tried to open the cabin windows. I added my strength to hers, but the sliding panels were immovable.

Then I remembered the Minetti in the glove compartment. The Minetti is effective only at short range; its bullets are minuscule slivers of metal. But its magazine holds a hundred rounds. I took the little gun and, firing in short bursts, stitched an oblong of perforations in the tough, transparent plastic. At the third blow from the butt of my heavier weapon it sagged outwards. Elspeth waited until I had put on my own dustshoes, then clambered carefully out of the opening. I followed her.

Hand in hand, with careful, sliding footsteps, always alert for the first, fatal trickle of dust over the rim of a shoe, we walked slowly towards the dome.

Chapter Twenty-two

THERE WERE cupolas on top of the Fergus dome; they looked like pimples on the gleaming hide of some great, sluggish beast. From some of them protruded the snouts of automatic weapons, from others antennae of various kinds sprouted. I saw that a pair of the guns swivelled slowly to cover and to follow us, that some kind of scanner did the same. I hoped that Fergus would not press the wrong button, and said as much.

"Not to worry, Johnnie," said Elspeth. "Father can see who we are now."

And then the old man's voice crackled out of the helmet phones. "Elspeth! What's wrong? I've been trying to raise you on your sled radio."

"It got slightly shot up," she said dryly. "And before that there was considerable interference."

"I told you to be careful," he said petulantly.

"We were careful," she told him. "And now, Father, will you please be quiet? We have to concentrate on walking."

"As you say, my dear," he grumbled.

We concentrated on walking. The dustshoes were not as hard to manage as skies, and for that I was thankful. A misadventure on these ungainly contraptions could well mean a particularly unpleasant and protracted form of death. So, carefully, carefully, we slid forward, wanting to hurry to the airlock that had opened at the base of the dome but not daring to do so.

I heaved a sigh of relief as Elspeth clumped into the little compartment, another one as I followed her. We stood there in a close embrace — or as close an embrace as was permitted by our frustrating suits — and watched the outer door shut, watched the needle of the pressure gauge on the wall climb slowly to atmospheric pressure. We threw up the visors of our helmets then and contrived a not very satisfactory kiss. While we were so engaged the inner door opened and Fergus stood there watching us. After his third cough we realized that he was there.

"Father," said Elspeth, disengaging herself without haste, "this is Mr Petersen."

He looked at me with faded blue eyes set in a leathery, wrinkled face under bushy white brows. He grinned frostily. He said, "It seems obvious, my dear, that you and Mr Petersen have already been introduced."

I returned his stare, not knowing quite what to make of him. Mores vary considerably throughout the galaxy and some astoundingly archaic ideas regarding the honour of female relatives still persist.

He thrust out a gnarled, stained hand. "Welcome aboard, Petersen. You took long enough getting here."

I returned his grasp. I said, "And we were slightly delayed at the finish by some friends of yours — post office employees."

Elspeth's bold, hard front was crumbling. She said, "It was horrible. There were three of them, three of the rocket sleds that they use for surface mail. They had guns and they tried to stop us."

The old man's face was sober. He said, "I knew, when it was too late, what was going to happen. I . . . I remembered. But I had known, before then, that the pair of you would reach the dome safely. I tried to warn you, Elspeth. I tried to call you on the radio. When there was no reply I began to wonder if the pattern had been broken."

"The pattern?" I demanded. Suddenly I was angry with this old fool. "What sort of father do you call yourself, letting your daughter go out to face attack by armed gangsters? To see men burning to death and drowning in the dust?"

He smiled wearily. "You don't understand, Petersen. You don't understand yet. And I don't understand, either, why it was essential that you come to Wenceslaus, imperative that you come to my dome. But I shall understand."

"All part of your blasted pattern, I suppose?"

"All part of *the* pattern," he corrected me.

"And we stand here to argue," cried Elspeth with a spurious gaiety, "still in our suits, when we have comfortable rooms waiting for us to use. And you, Johnnie, said that you were famished. Don't you want a meal and a drink?"

I fell in with her assumed mood. "I want a drink, a meal, and a drink," I said. "Also a shower. My feet are squelching in the sweat that's gathered in the boots of this damned suit."

"Good. Then I'll take you to your room."

Fergus led the way from the airlock chamber. I tried to forget the girl who was walking by my side, tried, in the best Sherlock Holmes tradition, to see and to observe. After all, I had been sent out from Carinthia to get inside this dome by hook or by crook, and the fact that I was inside it by its owner's invitation did not relieve me of my obligations.

Being inside the larger dome that was Pilsen had been like being inside a vast, fantastic conservatory. Being inside this one was like, at first, being inside a ship. There was a level in which were the hydroponics tanks. There was even the familiar whine of a Mannschenn Drive unit coming from somewhere. And in Pilsen the sobbing of pumps and whirr of fans had not been obtrusive; here no attempt had been made to mute or muffle the noise of essential machinery.

And then the resemblance to a ship was suddenly gone.

We entered, through a thick, heavily insulated door, a chamber in which the air struck cold on our exposed faces. All around us were cages, and in every cage was a small animal that I recognized as a Carinthian mountain cat. They were pretty little beasts, thickly furred, the pelts displaying a wide variety of coloration and patterning. Each of them was soundly asleep. Fergus picked up a long stick and went along a line of cages, prodding the inmates. None of them as much as stirred."

"Hibernation," he said. "These animals were brought out from the winter hemisphere and have been maintained in winter conditions."

"But they can be awakened?" I said, interested in spite of myself.

"Of course." He paused, seemed lost in thought, seemed to be trying to remember something. He went on, "I could remove one of these cats, put it in a warm room, and it would awaken. Or I have done so. Or I will do so." He paused again. "But there's this damned element of compulsion. And when did I initiate the cycle?"

He was interrupted by a sudden, mewing cry. We all of us turned, saw that one of the animals, one that had been poked and prodded as thoroughly as its companions, had awakened. It paced up and down in its cage like a tiny, subtly misproportioned tiger, its gaudy fur standing on end as a protection against the cold.

"Don't panic," muttered Fergus irritably. "Don't panic. You'll soon be somewhere warm." He turned to his daughter, "Elspeth! The time!"

She looked at the large clock on one of the walls. "It's 2203," she said.

"Hmm, 2203. Remember that carefully."

He grasped a handle at one end of the cages — it was, I saw, built on its own little trolley — and started to push it out of the room. Elspeth ran ahead of him and opened another insulated door. We passed through an airlock — or a heatlock? — into another compartment full of cages. The smell here was heavy and sickening. The snarlings and mewing of the mountain cats made speech almost impossible.

"You see," shouted Fergus, "that this one is the only one with tiger markings. And take a note of the number of his cage. Number 403. But he must be fed and watered."

He filled the drinking bowl in the cage from a hose, then opened a locker in the wall and took from it a piece of meat which he dropped through a trap. The animal lapped thirstily, then abandoned the water as soon as it saw or smelled the food. Its table manners were not of the best.

"He's not hibernating now!" shouted Fergus, his voice barely audible above the clamour of the other cats who, seeing their companion being fed, were resenting noisily this favouritism.

"It's time that *we* had something to eat," said Elspeth pointedly during a lull in the uproar.

"Yes, yes, my dear. But I have to show Mr Petersen what this is all about. And don't forget the time. I was 2203, wasn't it? And don't forget the cage number."

We followed him into yet a third room containing animals. But it was not the animals that first caught my attention. To one side of the place was a machine which I had always feared. There, whining disturbingly, was the gleaming complexity of a Mannschenn Drive unit, the smoothly spinning, ever-presessing gyroscopes, the shining wheels that tumbled. Tumbled, drawing eye and thought into a weirdly distorted continuum that seemed always on the point of vanishing into that less-than-nothingness — or greater-than-infinity? — and that somehow never did. I looked away from it hastily, but not before I had seen that mounted upon the time-twisting device was an oddly convoluted column, a Mobius Strip in three dimensions — or four? a Carlotti Beacon antenna. It was a fantastic rig that didn't, that couldn't make sense. Or did it make the wrong kind of sense?

"Don't look at it," warned Fergus.

"I've been in deep space!" I snapped.

"Then you should know better than to look. If you must look at something, look at the cages."

I looked at the cages.

There didn't seem to be anything odd about them. But what was odd was that the mountain cats inside them should be sleeping so soundly, even though the temperature of the room was uncomfortably warm. The animals, like those in the hibernatorium, could not be aroused by any amount of poking and prodding. Fergus said, "You could use anti-hibernine on these and it would have no effect. Do you want a demonstration?"

"Good. Now, Mr Petersen, would you mind going back and getting that cage with our tiger-striped friend? Number 403."

"Father," complained Elspeth, "is all this necessary?"

The face that he turned to her was bleak. He said, "It may not be necessary, but —"

"Don't go, Johnnie!" she cried.

I stood there hesitantly.

"I remember now," whispered Fergus. "*I* went —"

128

"*Will* go," she almost snapped.

We watched the old man as he left us, as he returned wheeling the cage with the snarling animal. He pushed it into a circle marked on the smooth, polished plastic of the floor. I saw that the Carlotti Beacon antenna, like the barrel of some fantastic gun, was pointed at the centre of the circle.

Fergus left it there, went to a complex switchboard. As he worked at it the whining of the Mannschenn Drive unit became almost supersonic. I wanted to look again at those devilish gyroscopes, but dared not, kept my regard fixed on Fergus and listened to the frenzied yowling of the mountain cat.

"Random setting!" screamed the old man. "Random setting!"

He gave a wheel a vicious twist, stood back from the switchboard. The wheel, that should have gone on spinning for minutes, slowed and stopped almost immediately. Fergus extended what looked like an impossibly long arm, snapped down a switch. The caterwauling of the animal ceased abruptly.

"The time," said Fergus in a normal voice.

I looked at the wall clock. It registered 2235. Fergus beckoned me to the switchboard, pointed to the dial behind the wheel that he had spun at random. *Minutes*, read the lettering, and the pointer had come to rest on 32.

I found myself doing mental arithmetic: 2235 − 2203 = 32.

I looked away from the dial to the mountain cat in its cage, at the tiger-striped beast in a deep sleep like that of the hibernation from which it had been somehow aroused. Or a deeper sleep?

"It's not dead," said Fergus tiredly. "It's not dead, but it cannot be awakened. It can be destroyed, but never awakened." There was a quality of desperation in his voice. "And time is running out."

Chapter Twenty-three

I AWOKE with a start, to the disturbing conviction that something was wrong. But the familiar sounds almost lulled me to sleep again — the thin, high keening of the interstellar drive, the sobbing pumps, the throbbing fans.

But there were other sounds.

There was someone breathing gently. I held my own breath for a few seconds, established the fact that it was not my own respiration to which I was listening. I moved uneasily in the bed and felt a woman's body, soft yet firm, warm, smooth, against my own. I began to remember.

"Ilona . . ." I whispered.

She made a little sound that was almost a purr.

But there were other sounds.

There was the ticking of a clock. There was, disconcertingly, a sudden outbreak of snarling screams that was not very distant. *The mountain cats*, I thought. *The mountain cats?* I asked myself.

Then there was this business of a gravitational field. A ship running under interstellar drive is, of necessity, in free fall. But we were not in free fall. There was no webbing to hold us in the bed. The bed, not a narrow ship's bunk.

I groped for the switch of the bedside lamp that we had left burning until, exhausted, we had drifted into a deep sleep. I could remember, now, having summoned my last reserves of energy to turn that light off. I pressed the switch. The soft, amber light was kind to my eyes. It was reflected from her tumbled, red-gold hair against the white pillow, from her smooth shoulder, from the creamy curve of her back.

Red-gold hair?

"Elspeth . . ." I said, very softly, remembering.

"Mmm?"

Elspeth, I thought.

Elspeth and her father, and this fantastic dome on the surface of this fantastic satellite, and the fantastic demonstration that I had witnessed . . . *And what*, I asked myself, *did it all add up to?* Well, I would tell Steve, or his Central Intelligence bosses, what I had seen and what I had heard. They could pick whatever bones they liked out of it. And what I had found for myself I would keep. To have and to hold. It all, I thought, comes right in the end.

But Ilona. . . .

Damn Ilona!

Elspeth stirred into full wakefulness. "Johnnie," she murmured. "Johnnie. . . ." And then she kissed me. She pulled away from me. "Johnnie, you're looking so grim. Can't you sleep?"

"It's a shame to sleep," I told her. "When I'm sleeping I can't appreciate you."

She said, "I like to be appreciated."

I said, "I like to appreciate you."

She said, "Then appreciate me."

Smooth she was, and soft, and open to me, and together we allowed ourselves to be carried along by the mounting tide of our passion. Then, suddenly, she stiffened in my arms. For a little while I persisted, but moving gently, afraid that I was hurting her. Then I heard what she had heard, the stridency of a bell. She said bitterly, "This living in a damned fortress under siege!"

Reluctantly I let her go, watched her almost run to the connecting door between our rooms. That noisy alarm was insistent, urgent, but it seemed to me to be of the utmost importance that I impress upon my memory for always this vision of her slim, lovely nakedness. I felt — was it premonition? was it memory? — that something incalculably precious was going out of my life.

I got out of the bed, hurried to the shower cabinet where Elspeth had hung my clothes to dry after giving them a much needed wash. I buckled the belt with the holstered automatic over my shirt and slacks. The magazine of the pistol was empty, but I hoped that Fergus

131

would be able to supply me with ammunition. After all, as Elspeth had said, the dome was a fortress and, as such, should be able to boast a well-stocked armoury.

She was waiting for me in the corridor outside our rooms. Together we hurried down ramps and along other corridors, coming at last to a large compartment that I had not seen before — or had I? It was disturbingly familiar. The curved outer wall of it was completely transparent and through this huge window I could see the dust sea and the smooth horizon, the horizon that now bisected the blazing orb of the setting sun. In the middle distance there was a splash of scarlet — another of the post office rocket sleds? — and halfway between it and the dome were two slowly moving figures.

Fergus looked up bad-temperedly from a control panel, gestured towards a large desk the top of which was littered with books, papers and mathematical instruments. "I was close to the solution," he complained. "I know that I was close. And now these people. . . ."

"Who are they?" I asked.

"How should I know, Petersen? All I know is that the alarm went off, and then there was somebody jabbering on the radio demanding a parley." He snorted. "A parley? Are they playing at soldiers?"

"They've been playing at soldiers already," I told him. "And playing rough. But this solution . . .?"

"Yes. The solution. The solution to the problem of stasis, or pseudo-stasis, when the transfer takes place. It's vitally important, Petersen. And now, this interruption. . . ."

The trudging figures were closer.

"Hadn't you better to go the airlock, Father?" suggested Elspeth.

"No," he snapped. "They may have weapons in that sled of theirs. I prefer to stay here, where I can control my own artillery." He turned to me. "You can make yourself useful, Petersen."

"All right," I said.

"Do you know the way, Johnnie?" asked Elspeth.

"No."

"Then I'll come with you," she said.

As she led the way I noticed that there was a slight bulge in each side pocket of her shorts. So she was armed. So she was used to leaping from bed and dressing quickly at the call to action stations. The realization made me feel a little better, a little less frustrated. And, in any case, I knew very well by this time that the people who were after Fergus's secret played for keeps; it was nice to know that the members of the Fergus family played the same way.

We came to the inner door of the airlock and I stood back while the girl operated the simple controls. I saw her looking through the port in the door, heard her say, "They're in." I watched the needle of the gauge creep to *one atmosphere*, and then the inner door opened.

Two men came into the dome, both of them in suits with fishbowl-type helmets within which their faces were clearly visible. One of them was a stranger. The other....

"Mr Petersen," he said coldly, nodding to me.

"Mr Maleter," I said.

"You'd have been better advised to have gone out to the Rim while you had the chance," he told me.

"Should I?" I countered.

He dismissed me with a contemptuous glance, turned to Elspeth. "Miss Fergus, please take us to your father."

She looked at me. "Shall I?"

"Yes," I said. I drew my automatic. "Yes. But, first of all, I suggest that these gentlemen leave their armament in the airlock."

Maleter shrugged. He asked coldly, "Is this necessary, my man?"

"It is," I said.

He and his companion unbuckled the belts that they wore outside their spacesuits, let them and the heavy holsters fall to the floor. I nodded to Elspeth and she started to lead the way. I brought up the rear. It seemed a long way to the room in which we had left Fergus, and for every inch of it I was conscious of the emptiness of the magazine of my pistol. I was glad that the others couldn't see my face.

Fergus turned away from his control panel as we entered the big compartment, glared at the two intruders. He held a machine pistol in his right hand and looked as though he would welcome the chance to use it. "Yes?" he demanded.

"I am Maleter," stated the branch manager of Trans-Galactic Clippers. "And this is Postmaster General Greusz. In happier days he was General Greusz."

"Maleter?" repeated Fergus. "Iron Man Maleter?"

"That is the name by which I was known on Si Kiang."

"What do you want?" asked Fergus coldly.

"Need you ask?" parried the other. "But I assure you, Mr Fergus, that I am willing to pay, and handsomely, for what you have to sell."

"I am a rich man," Fergus told him. "But even if I were not, I should not sell to you."

"You are a scientist," said Maleter. "Would you not welcome proof that the cycle can be broken?"

"The cycle is unbreakable," said Fergus bleakly.

"When there is determination," Maleter said, "anything may be broken. When there is determination, combined with fore-knowledge. Or memory? After all, it would not be hard. It would require only the trial and execution of certain fleet commanders before they committed the acts of treason that made them criminals, deserving the ultimate penalty." He added, "But a trial, of course, would not be necessary."

"How much do you know?" asked Fergus. "How much do you know?"

"Not enough," admitted Maleter frankly. "If I knew everything I should not be obliged to bargain for your services. This much I do know: you have perfected a device, incorporating the Mannschenn Drive and the Carlotti Beacon, whereby the consciousness of any being may be sent back in time. I know, too, that any being so treated is trapped in a time cycle, that he, or she, or it, must play over and over the sequence of events between the transfer points. And I know that there is no consciousness after the latter transfer point; that the body only survives, but as a mere, mindless hulk." He paused. "Am I correct?"

"You have a reasonably efficient intelligence service," grunted Fergus.

"Thank you. Now, Fergus, I have learned that you, and your daughter, and perhaps this man Petersen, are approaching the end of the sequence, the transfer point. You are worried about it. You wish that there were some means by which you could avoid being trapped again in the cycle, some means to escape the pseudo-death that is creeping up on you all. But you'll never escape it by your own efforts, Fergus. You're a clever man; a genius, if you wish. But you haven't the guts. I — and I am not boasting — have. Send me back, Fergus. Send me back to some time just prior to the naval mutiny, and I'll break the cycle for you. I shall remember enough. Could I ever forget my hate for Admiral Chung Lee, for Commodore Vishinsky, for the other traitors who ruined me?"

"They were not criminals," said Fergus. "You were, and you are."

"I neither was nor am, Mr Fergus. I was unlucky. Or, perhaps unwise in that I trusted those who were essentially untrustworthy. And you can sell me the chance to cancel this unluckiness, or this unwisdom, to punish before the crime, to achieve a victory that will make subsequent defeat impossible."

"No," said Fergus.

Maleter turned to look at Elspeth. He said softly, "You love your daughter, Mr Fergus. You are not demonstrative and you allow her to run into danger, but you love her in your own strange manner. I tell you, Mr Fergus, that if you do not accede to my reasonable requests she, and this spacepup of hers, will be exposed to the gravest danger."

"You tried that before, Maleter," I growled. I turned to

his companion. "And how many of your brave postmen bit the dust general? Or should I address you as Postmaster General?"

"Many of my men, Petersen," said Greusz coldly, "are, like myself, soldiers from Flammarion's Cluster."

"Rocket Brigade, no doubt," I sneered.

"However did you guess?" he retorted with a wintry smile.

"You are wasting time, general," Maleter told him. "Time, as we well know, means nothing to our young friend Petersen, but is a factor to be considered by those of us who are important in galactic affairs." He turned to Fergus. "And time, Mr Fergus, is running out."

"I know," said Fergus. "I know."

"I will be honest with you," Maleter went on. 'Time has almost run out for me. I have nothing to lose. A strong detachment of armed police is already on its way from Carinthia to Wenceslaus to place me under arrest. There was the sabotage of *Moonmaiden*, together with one or two subsequent events. Certain busybodies have succeeded in linking my name with these happenings. So, Mr Fergus, you will either help me or take the consequences." He smiled almost happily. "That is the beauty of capital punishment. One can be executed only once, no matter how many murders he has committed."

I looked at the two men. They were unarmed, but they were desperate. I looked at Fergus. He was holding his machine pistol as though he knew how to use it. I looked at Elspeth. She had a deadly little Minetti in each slim, capable hand.

"Get out," said Fergus. "Get out. And you, Elspeth, call the Pilsen police and tell them about these threats."

"Just as a matter of interest," drawled Greusz, "did you succeed in reporting that unfortunate fracas out on the desert?" He grinned. "A postmaster general may not be as glamorous as a general, but he has absolute control over all means of communication."

"Get out," said Fergus, in almost a whisper.

Suddenly, shockingly, the machine pistol chattered. Greusz paled, stared down at his foot, at the neat holes stitched in the polished plastic of the floor around the outline of his boot. He said stiffly to Maleter, "I suggest, sir, that we withdraw."

Maleter said, "You will regret this, Fergus."

Fergus said again, "Get out."

This time it was I who led the way to the airlock, with Elspeth bringing up the rear. When we reached the little compartment I hastily scooped up the two belts with their holstered pistols, then moved smartly to one side. I should have used one of the automatics, but shooting down unarmed men was never one of my specialities. I watched in silence as the two of them strapped on their dustshoes, dropped the visors of their helmets. And then the inner door closed on them. When they were outside the chamber Elspeth actuated the locking device of the outer door.

We returned in silence to the control room, watched through the huge window the pair of them walking slowly over the dust to the scarlet sled, their shadows distorted and enormously elongated. Fergus was peering into a screen that served as a gun sight; his heavy automatics, I knew, were ready to blast the vehicle at the first signs of hostile action.

But there was none.

Maleter and his general climbed into the sled. There was a puff of smoke and a flash of flame from its rear and then the thing was under way, diminishing swiftly, vanishing over the curvature of the near horizon.

Chapter Twenty-four

"CAN'T YOU get through?" demanded Fergus.

"No," replied his daughter shortly, looking up from the useless radio.

"I'm surprised that they haven't attacked by now," I said, lowering the binoculars through which I had been scanning the empty horizon. "But they may be waiting for dark. The sun's not far to go."

"It will make no difference," Fergus told me. "My radar is highly efficient."

"And soon the ship will be dropping down from Carinthia," I said, "with the armed police." I laughed. "Policemen versus postmen! A civil war in the Civil Service! But what really amazes me is the idea of building up the post office into a private army. And where did they get their weapons from?"

"They got them," said Fergus. "And that's all that matters."

"Ex-dictator sets up in business again on a new world," I said, "with a crystal gazing machine to help him."

"It's not crystal gazing," snapped Fergus. "And I have never claimed to be able to see into the future."

"Then what are you doing?" I asked.

He looked at me and said slowly, "The executive officers of Trans-Galactic clippers are even more stupid than they were when I was a spaceman. You saw that experiment with the mountain cat, Petersen. You heard all that Maleter said. I suppose that you've read a few reports. Are you incapable of adding two and two to make four?"

"No."

"Then add two and two."

"Time travel," I said. "But I still think that it's impossible."

"It's not impossible. Time travel — one way only. With

limitations. Limitations of which Mr. Maleter is fully aware."

"Not into the future?"

"No."

"And not physically?"

"No. And I'll tell you the third limitation, as you'll never work it out for yourself. You can travel back in time only to a period during which you were affected by the temporal precession field of a Mannschenn Drive unit. Which means to a time during which you were proceeding from point A to point B in an interstellar ship. Do you understand?"

"No, I don't," I said frankly.

He snorted. "Then think about it sometime when you haven't got more pressing problems on your mind. Meanwhile, just take for granted what I've said, that your mentality, your personality, can be sent back in time." He was warming to his theme. "One trouble is this. You can't remember everything. You *do* remember all the things that you must remember to maintain the sequence. As for the rest — you remember some of it, but always too late for you to do anything to break the cycle. In my cycle, for example, I remember enough to make two or three fortunes by investment. But I don't remember, until too late, the catastrophe that kills my wife. Each time round I try to avert it, but never soon enough."

"And Maleter hopes that he will remember enough to be able to deal with the top brass of his navy before the mutiny?"

"Didn't he say so?"

"He did."

"But if he's been trapped in a time cycle, he must, by now, realize the futility of it."

"He's not trapped in the cycle yet. Perhaps he never will be. You, for example, have been drawn into it only recently. But as long as the cycle is maintained, others will be drawn into it."

"A cosmic carousel," I said.

"It's no laughing matter," he snapped.

"I wasn't laughing. But what about the mountain cats? How do they come into it? Are they in a cycle too?"

"They are."

"And what happens to them when they reach the transfer point? When their intelligences, hibernating or alert, are sent back in time?"

"That's what frightens me," he said quietly. "They are drained of . . . of some vital essence. They are not dead, but neither are they alive. And when your own time comes, when we reach the end of the sequence. . . ."

"But it needn't come."

"It must come. How could I be what I am today, a rich man, if I had not been able to use my memories of stock market fluctuations?"

"If you can make, you can break," I said.

He laughed bitterly. "I wish it were as easy as that."

"What was it that Maleter told you?" I asked. "That you hadn't the guts to break the Cycle —" I raised a hand to check his angry outburst. "Oh, you have the guts all right. But have you the desire, a strong enough desire? In your heart of hearts you know that this cycle gives you all you want — the money and the freedom to engage in fascinating research. It's immortality of a kind. A strong love, or a strong hate, might tip the scales. (Maleter, for example, has a strong hate.) But be honest with yourself. Have you ever loved, or hated, strongly enough? You love your daughter, and every time round you save her. But did you love your wife?"

For a moment I feared that he was going to strike me, and knew that if he did so I should deserve it. Then his hand dropped and a twisted smile distorted his features. He whispered, "You're right, Petersen. I hated the bitch. I knew that she was deceiving me. I knew that she deserved to die that night."

"Father!" There was shocked incredulity in Elspeth's voice.

And then another voice, Maleter's voice, crackled from

the speaker of the transceiver.

"Maleter calling Fergus. Maleter calling Fergus. Come in, Fergus. Come in."

The old man snatched the microphone. "What do you want?"

"You, Fergus. And your apparatus."

"You've already had my answer."

"Look out of that big, beautiful window of yours," sneered the voice from the radio.

We looked out. We scanned the horizon for the flashes of scarlet that would betray the approach of the post office rocket sleds. We saw nothing. And then, barely short of the dome, the dust erupted into towering geysers that hung against the dark sky for long seconds, that hung against the sky and slowly tumbled and crumbled about themselves, leaving miniature ring craters that filled even as we watched.

"The first salvo," said Maleter.

"Those damned mail rockets," I swore.

"Did I hear the spacepuppy mention mail rockets?" pleasantly inquired the disembodied voice. "He cannot be wrong all the time; the law of averages allows him a small percentage of correct guesses. That was one of them."

Fergus pressed a button and a sheet of metal slid up to cover the huge window. While it was still in motion Maleter said, "The second salvo will miss too, but it will be a very near miss."

We didn't see the second salvo, but we felt it. The dome shook and quivered, heeled like a surface ship in a ground swell. From the animal quarters came a cacophony of screams and snarls.

"Well, Fergus?" asked Maleter.

"You're a military man," said Fergus quietly. "You know, as well as an occasional student of military affairs like myself knows, that artillery can destroy, but it can never take and occupy."

"The ground forces," said Maleter, "take and occupy when the opposition has been battered to surrender or wiped out. But, fascinating as I find this discussion of strategy and tactics, I regret that time will not permit me to pursue it further. Do you surrender?"

Fergus was making frantic gestures to his daughter, seemed to be climbing into an invisible pair of trousers, donning an imaginary hat. Elspeth looked at him in bewilderment at first, then nodded. She walked quickly out of the room.

"Do you surrender?"

"What are your terms?" asked Fergus.

"Unconditional surrender, of course. Unconditional surrender, and the utmost co-operation. And you will leave the dome, all three of you, before the first of my vehicles is within range of your guns. I'll not risk treachery a second time."

Elspeth returned, carrying three suits. Silently we climbed into them.

"I am waiting," said Maleter. "Unless I receive an answer before I have counted to ten —"

"The answer," Fergus said, "is no."

"All right, you old fool. You asked for it."

I saw that Fergus and Elspeth had shut their helmet visors. I followed suit, but I could still hear the screaming from the cat cages, found time to feel sorry for the poor brutes. And then the third salvo landed. It hit the side of the dome squarely, clanging like a monstrous hammer smashing an enormous bell. The concussion knocked us off our feet. Sprawled prone on the floor, one arm flung in a futile gesture of protection over Elspeth, I saw that the metal shield over the window was buckled inwards, that a torrent of grey dust was pouring in through the rents. There was the thin, high whistling of the last of the air escaping from the dome. When it ceased, the shrieking of the mountain cats had ceased also.

There was a voice yammering irritatingly in my helmet phones, over and over: "Petersen! Elspeth! The Mannschenn Drive room. Safer there. . . ." Fergus was back on his feet and was tugging at me frantically, and at last I was able to rise, almost to lose my footing again when the fourth salvo hit somewhere overhead.

Then I was trying to help Elspeth up from the floor. "Elspeth," I was saying. "Elspeth. . . ." But she neither replied nor moved. I managed to pick her up then, slung her over my shoulder, followed the old man as he staggered through the door and along the passageway. The dust was everywhere, welling up through cracks in the flooring like a sluggish fluid, hampering my feet.

I lost count of the salvoes. Each one was felt now rather than heard. With each one the dome lurched and quivered; with each one the lights flickered and, along stretches of corridor, failed. Then, as we were passing through the room with the cages full of contorted, furry bodies, there was a lull in the firing. Maleter's voice came through on the suit radio frequency, "Had enough, Fergus?"

"Come within the range of my guns and find out!" snarled the engineer.

Those same guns, I thought, must be twisted, useless wreckage by now.

The firing resumed.

Chapter Twenty-five

"ELSPETH . . ." I muttered. "Elspeth. . . . She — she's dead."

I looked long and stupidly at the airpipe that had been severed by a flying shard of metal. I did not want to look at her face again. Her death may have been fast, but it had not been pleasant.

"I know," whispered her father. "I — I remembered it,

when it was too late. But we shall see her again, Petersen. Or we will have seen her. But always this tragedy at the end of the cycle. Always. . . ."

He stood there, his face turned away from me, staring into the spinning, gleaming, ever-precessing complexity of the drive, a small, hunched figure, dwarfed by the machinery of which he was, nonetheless, master. He staggered as the floor lurched under him, staggered and almost slipped on the encroaching tide of dust. The dome, I realized, was foundering like a surface ship, would soon be sinking deep into the dust sea, and Maleter and his men would find nothing but faint, fast-flattening ripples, would have gained nothing from their orgy of destruction. Retribution would catch up with them, but that was small comfort to us.

"Petersen! Petersen!" Fergus was speaking urgently.

"Yes?"

"Stand in the circle."

"It's covered with dust," I said stupidly.

"You know where to stand."

I shuffled to where he was pointing and stood there, hypnotized by the spinning, precessing wheels, by the slowly turning, convoluted column of the Carlotti Beacon antenna. I was vaguely aware that Fergus was at his control panel, that he was plugging into a socket a switch at the end of a length of flex. Of course, I thought. Of course, he'll be sending himself back next, and he'll have to use some sort of remote control . . . .

"Petersen," he was saying. "Try to break the cycle. Next time round, try to break the cycle. . . ."

He twisted the wheel and this time it went on spinning for a long time, finally coming to rest. He pressed the switch.

I awoke with a start, to the frightening conviction that something was dreadfully wrong. I tried to remember the evil dream that must have been responsible for my uneasiness. For everything was normal — the thin, high keening of the interstellar drive that is so much of a spaceman's life, the sobbing pumps, the whining fans.

But there was another sound.

There was someone breathing gently. I held my own breath for a few seconds, established the fact that it was not my own respiration to which I was listening. I moved uneasily in the bunk, hampered slightly by the webbing, and immediately felt a woman's body, soft yet firm, warm, smooth, against my own. The situation, which I had somehow been convinced was dreadfully wrong, was beautifully right. I groped for the switch of the bunkside lamp that we had left burning, until exhausted, we had drifted into a deep sleep. I could remember, now, summoning my last reserves of energy to turn that light off.

I pressed the switch. The soft, amber light was kind to my eyes. It was reflected from her sleek, shining auburn hair against the white pillow, from her smooth shoulder, from the golden curves of her slender back, from the naked loveliness that was somehow enhanced by the illusion of bonds presented by the light webbing.

"Elspeth . . ." I whispered.

She replied with a sound that was half grunt and half purr, turned over sleepily, breasts and thighs pressing against me, her parted lips lifted to mine.

Elspeth. I thought.

Elspeth?

"Ilona . . .?" I whispered.

"Mmmm?"

"Ilona. . . ." I kissed her. "Ilona. . . ."

She stirred into full wakefulness. "Johnnie," she murmured, and returned my kiss. "Johnnie. . . . You're looking so worried. Can't you sleep?"

"It's a shame to sleep," I told her. "When I'm sleeping I can't appreciate you."

"She said, "I like to be appreciated."

I said, "I like to appreciate you."

She said, "Then appreciate me."

Later, as we were talking drowsily, she said, "Johnnie, it will be so much better when we have our night together in New Prague. It will be so much better with euphorine . . . ."

Euphorine?

A little, warning bell rang at the back of my mind.

Euphorine?

And another bell rang — the telephone. It was the third officer giving me the one-bell call, the quarter hour's grace before I was due on watch. "Yes," I mumbled into the mouthpiece of the instrument. "Yes, I'm awake. I'll be right up."

Reluctantly I slid from under the webbing, off the bunk, thrusting my feet into my magnetic-soled sandals. I stood and looked down at Ilona, at the slender, golden grace of her.

And . . . .

And there was the memory of an insistent alarm bell, and of how I had watched from the bed the lovely nakedness of the girl as she hurried towards the door, the red-gold hair and creamy skin. . . .

Elspeth . . . .

Who was Elspeth?

"Petersen," he was saying. "Petersen. Try to break the cycle."

He twisted the wheel and it went on spinning for a long time, finally coming to rest. I saw his fingers tighten on the switch. "Hold it!" I cried.

I ran out of the circle, grabbed the wheel, exerted all my strength to try to twist it a further fraction of a turn counter clockwise. Somehow this time, this last time, the memories had come flooding back, all the memories, and with them the picture of Elspeth horridly dead inside her spacesuit. I knew what I had to do to break the cycle. I had to return in time to a period prior to my first night with Ilona; I had to avoid becoming entangled with her. And after that? After that I would have to play by ear, bearing in mind always the necessity of saving Elspeth.

But the wheel resisted all my efforts. My booted feet slipped on the encroaching dust. My gloved hands slipped on the wheel, lost their hold. And the pressure released, the wheel turned of itself, spinning clockwise.

As I scrambled back into the circle I saw Fergus press the switch. Desperately I wondered what the future would hold. But then, what future could there be in a shattered dome buried fathoms deep beneath the surface of the dust sea?

Chapter Twenty-six

THE CYCLE had been interfered with, but not broken. Time travel was possibly only on the temporal line between the two transfer points. But I had retained all my memories.

I was back in the control room with Fergus and Elspeth, looking out over the featureless desert beyond the horizon of which the scarlet post office sled had just vanished.

"If you can make, you can break," I was saying.

Fergus laughed bitterly. "I wish it were as easy as that."

"What was it that Maleter told you?" I asked. "That you hadn't the guts to break the cycle —" I raised a hand to check his angry outburst. "Oh, you have the guts all right. But have you the desire, a strong enough desire? In your heart of hearts you know that your cycle gives you all you want — money and the freedom to engage in fascinating research. It's immortality of a kind. But a strong love, or a strong hate, could tip the scales. (Maleter, for example, has that strong hate.) But be honest with yourself, Fergus. Have *you* ever loved, or hated, strongly enough? You love your daughter, and every time round you save her from that catastrophe on Earth's moon. Every time round you try to persuade me to break the cycle so that she can be saved from the painful death that awaits her here. *But did you love your wife?*"

For a moment I feared that he was going to strike me, and then knew that he would not. His hand dropped and a bitter, twisted smile distorted his features. He whispered, "You're right, Petersen. I hated the bitch. I knew that she was deceiving me. I knew that she deserved to die that night."

"Father!" There was shocked incredulity in Elspeth's voice.

And another voice, Maleter's crackled from the speaker of the transceiver.

"Maleter calling Fergus. Maleter calling Fergus. Come in, Fergus. Come in."

The old man snatched the microphone. "What do you want?"

"You, Fergus. And your apparatus."

"You've already had my answer."

"Look out of that big, beautiful window of yours," sneered the voice from the radio.

The others looked. I did not. I reached over and switched off the radio; that microphone, I knew, was far too sensitive.

"Elspeth," I ordered. "Spacesuits. We're getting out."

I turned to see, barely short of the dome, the dust erupting into towering geysers that hung against the dark sky for long seconds, that hung against the dark sky and then slowly tumbled and crumbled about themselves, leaving miniature ring craters that filled even as I watched.

"The first salvo," I remarked. "Elspeth, hurry with those suits!"

As she was running from the room Fergus pressed a button and a sheet of metal slid up to cover the huge window. No sooner was it in place than the second salvo landed. We didn't see it, but we felt it. The dome shook and quivered, heeled like a surface ship in a ground swell. From the animal quarters came a cacophony of screams and snarls.

"I think that it's time that we aren't here," I said.

"We can't leave the dome," said Fergus tiredly. "Not now. Not at this stage, with our time almost run out. We are tied to the machine."

I replied with an obscene monosyllable and would have said more had not Elspeth returned with the suits. Silently we climbed into them. I snapped shut the faceplate of my helmet but could still hear the screaming from the cat cages. I felt sorry for the poor brutes. I nudged the switch of my suit radio with my chin, heard Maleter's voice: "Do you surrender?" I gestured to Fergus, clapping a hand over my mouth, outside my helmet. He nodded in comprehension.

"I am waiting," said Maleter. "Unless I receive an answer before I have counted to ten. . . ."

I caught Elspeth's hand, started to run with her from the control room. Fergus followed. We were out of the compartment when the third salvo landed. It hit the side of the dome squarely, clanging like a monstrous hammer smashing an enormous bell. The concussion knocked us off our feet. I remembered that the metal shield of the window had been buckled inwards, that a torrent of grey dust was pouring through the rents. I heard again the thin, high whistling of the last of the air escaping from the dome. When it ceased, the shrieking of the mountain cats ceased also.

There was a voice yammering irritatingly in my helmet phones, over and over: "Petersen! Elspeth! The Mannschenn Drive room. Safer there. . . ." Fergus was back on his feet, turning at me frantically, and at last I was able to rise, almost losing my footing again as the fourth salvo hit somewhere overhead.

Then I was trying to help Elspeth up from the floor. "Elspeth," I was saying. "Elspeth. . . ." When she neither replied nor moved a sensation of sickening futility swept over me. I bent to pick her up, was slinging her over my shoulder when she stirred, started to struggle. I heard her say, "It's all right, Johnnie. I can navigate under my own steam." We followed the old man as he staggered along the passageway. The dust was everywhere, welling up through cracks in the plating like a sluggish fluid, hampering our feet.

Fergus turned sharply to the right, taking the way that would lead him to the interior of the dome and his precious apparatus. "No," I shouted. "Not that way! Come with us!"

He paused briefly, turned, shook his head, then started off again.

I caught Elspeth's arm, tried to pull her in the direction of the airlock. She broke free from me, ran after her father. I followed them, but somehow could never catch up to them. It was like running through a nightmare — the nightmare of the dome lurching and shuddering under the impact of the salvoes, of the flickering and failing lights, of the cages with their furry, contorted bodies in the animal rooms.

I heard Maleter's voice on the suit radio frequency, "Had enough, Fergus?"

Nobody answered him.

Chapter Twenty-seven

FERGUS STOOD in the Mannschenn Drive room, his face turned away from us, staring into the spinning, gleaming ever-precessing complexity of the Drive, a small, hunched figure, dwarfed by the machinery of which he was, nonetheless, master — master? Was he the master?

Enlightenment came to me in a flash. He was a slave to

his machine and, at the same time, a slave to his own past, just as I, once I had been trapped in the cycle, was a slave to mine. This had always been the transfer point and it always would be the transfer point. But this time Elspeth was alive. The cycle could be broken.

Fergus staggered as the floor lurched under him, staggered and almost slipped on the encroaching tide of dust. The dome, I realized, was foundering like a holed surface ship, would soon be sinking deep into the dust sea, and Maleter and his men would find nothing but faint, fast-flattening ripples, would have gained nothing by their orgy of destruction. Retribution would catch up with them, but that would be small comfort to us.

"Elspeth!" Fergus was speaking urgently.

"Yes, father?"

"Stand in the circle."

"No!" I shouted.

"Stand in the circle," he repeated.

She broke away from me, shuffled slowly to where he was pointing and stood there, seemingly hypnotised by the spinning, precessing wheels, by the slowly turning, weirdly convoluted column of the Carlotti Beacon antenna. I was aware that Fergus was at his control panel, that he was plugging into a socket a switch at the end of a wandering lead. Of course, I thought. Of course, he'll be sending himself back after he's dealt with me, and he'll have to use some sort of remote control . . . .

Holding the switch in his left hand, he went to spin the controlling wheel with his right. "Stop!" I bawled. He hesitated. He muttered vaguely, "Petersen —"

"Break the cycle!" I snapped.

"What?" he asked stupidly.

Suddenly something happened within me. I took down from its rack on the wall a heavy wrench, flung it with all my strength into the whirling, precessing complex. There was the scream of shearing metal, a shrapnel-burst of sparks and fragments. For a microsecond — or for an eternity? — all my past life, my past lives, crowded in around me. There were the vivid memories of Ilona, and of Elspeth, and of others whom I had known long ago. But it was all more vivid than the most vivid memory.

And then. . . .

And then the past was utterly, irrevocably dead and gone.

"You've smashed it," Fergus was sobbing. "You've — you've killed it."

"Machines," I said, "cannot be killed; only broken."

I realized that Elspeth was clinging to me. I started to walk with her from the room. I said to Fergus, "You'd better come with us."

"No," he said. "No. The spares. There is still time to repair —"

"You'd better —"

"Leave him," said the girl softly, regretfully. "Leave him. This was his life. And with the doors shut this compartment will be reasonably dust-tight. Leave him. He still has the chance to regain his own kind of immortality." She whispered, "Goodbye, Father." He did not hear. Already he had dragged from a locker a new rotor to replace the one that had been smashed.

We did not go down. The airlock, we knew, must already be deep beneath the dust. We went up, Elspeth leading, to the top of the dome, to the gun turrets. The rocket salvoes were still pounding our citadel but were becoming less frequent. Soon, we knew, Maleter's forces would be closing in for the final assault, but they would be too late. The dome would be gone, sinking deeper and deeper, taking its secrets with it, and there was the possibility that Maleter, realizing this, would not investigate closely. It was a slim possibility, but it was a chance that we had to take.

The turret into which we made our way was smashed, its gun twisted beyond recognition. I consoled myself with the thought that artillery, unlike lightning, seldom strikes twice in the same place. By the last illumination from the sun's upper limb, the final sliver of light above the dark horizon, we saw that almost all the volume of the dome was now submerged, only the gun and radar cupolas projecting above the surface. One last rocket fell, well wide of us, and the column of dust it threw up was ruddily luminous in the glare of the exploding warhead.

We had no dustshoes, but flung towards us by that last explosion was a shallowly curved sheet of metal. It fell onto the small remaining exposed area of the dome, began to slide down to the dust. The broken stub of a radar scanner halted its progress. I scrambled out of the shattered turret, helped Elspeth out after me. Cautiously we slid towards the sheet of thin plating, eased it away from the obstruction. We slid it before us towards the surface of the dust sea, out onto the surface. It floated. Slowly, carefully, Elspeth transferred her weight to the makeshift raft. I followed her, and was no sooner aboard than, quite suddenly, the dome was gone, leaving only ripples that flattened as we watched.

We sat there in silence, as close to each other as our suits would allow. Once it seemed to me that I heard, over my suit radio, the familiar whine of a Mannschenn Drive unit and wondered if Fergus had succeeded in repairing and restarting his machine. But if he had, it was no longer any concern of ours. We heard nothing from Maleter.

And then, over the horizon, we saw the advancing searchlights of the rocket sleds, a line of impossibly bright stars at extremely low altitude. So this was it. Should we be better off, I wondered, if we went over the side of our raft? Would Maleter shoot us as soon as he came within range, or would he question us, thinking, mistakenly, that we knew the secret?

The orderly line of lights broke up, scattered. I could see explosions, streams of bright tracers. And I heard in my helmet phones a familiar voice, "Steve here, Johnnie. Steve here. Are you all right? Come in, please."

"We are all right," I said. "Come and get us."

And we waited there, happy in the knowledge that the past was gone, content to be facing the future together.